The cool wind blew back the hood of my sweatshirt and I didn't pull it up again. My hair would soon be in tangles, but it felt good blowing free.

Randy turned to face me and reached out to tuck a strand behind my ear. I started to put my hood back on, but he stopped me. "You look great with the ocean behind you and your hair flying," he said.

Our eyes met and held, and then he took my hands in his. Randy's eyes were exactly the color of the ocean. After what seemed like an eternity, he bent over and kissed my lips softly. I held my breath, hardly able to believe this was really happening. Then he pulled me into his arms, oblivious of the surfers below. I could feel my heart pounding against his, and I wished this moment could last forever.

Bantam titles in the Sweet Dreams series. Ask your bookseller for titles you have missed:

Sweet Dreams

Time Out for Love
June O'Connell

BANTAM BOOKS
NEW YORK • TORONTO • LONDON • SYDNEY • AUCKLAND

TIME OUT FOR LOVE
A BANTAM BOOK 0 553 29059 2

First publication in Great Britain

PRINTING HISTORY
Bantam edition published 1992

Sweet Dreams and its associated logo are registered trademarks of Bantam Books, a division of Bantam Doubleday Dell Publishing Group, Inc. Registered in U.S. Patent and Trademark Office and elsewhere.

Cover photo by Pat Hill

Bantam Books are published by Transworld Publishers Ltd., 61–63 Uxbridge Road, Ealing, London W5 5SA, in Australia by Transworld Publishers (Australia) Pty. Ltd., 15–23 Helles Avenue, Moorebank, NSW 2170, and in New Zealand by Transworld Publishers (N.Z.) Ltd., 3 William Pickering Drive, Albany, Auckland.

Printed and bound in Great Britain by Cox & Wyman Ltd., Reading, Berks.

To Michelle Buckman, Clark Johnson,
and Bee Thoma,
who while coaching my daughters
taught me so much about gymnastics

Chapter One

Not *again!*

I hit the mat under the balance beam with a smack and looked up at the ceiling of the American Gym Club, wondering if my new gymnastics routine would ever come out right. Even staying for a late practice hadn't helped. If things didn't start going better soon, I'd never be ready for the Elite championship.

Pulling myself up, I climbed back onto the beam. "What went wrong that time?" I asked my coach, Flip Lewis.

"You're not tired, are you?" he asked.

I groaned. "I've done this thing five hundred times tonight!"

"Just a couple more and we'll call it quits."

Taking a deep breath, I forced myself to concentrate and threw myself into another double-back aerial somersault. Landing hard, I did manage to get both feet to hit the beam. But again, I found myself flat on my back.

I didn't make any move to get up. "Maybe I'd make a better mattress tester than a gymnast."

Flip laughed and leaned over me. His red, curly hair sprang out from his painter's cap that had AWESOME spelled in large blue letters across the front. His aqua-blue eyes almost looked sun-bleached, but his fair skin gave every indication it would burn after ten minutes at the beach. I guess that's why he had a hard time understanding why I loved to spend my free time there. And who wouldn't? Living in southern California and *not* going to the beach would really be strange.

I pulled myself to a sitting position. "Can we quit now?"

Flip reached out his hand to help me up. "Let's try it one more time. You were so close."

This time I hopped on the beam with more enthusiasm. At least after this one last time, I could go home. I knew I shouldn't complain—Flip was always willing to stay late and give me extra help. But sometimes I wondered if it was worth all the effort. To accomplish my goal of becoming an Elite gymnast, I'd had to give up all school activities. That had been okay when I was younger, but now that I was a sophomore at Seagate High School, I had a few doubts.

Pushing the negative thoughts away, I lifted my chin. Gymnastics had been my life for eight years and I wasn't going to stop now that my goal was within reach.

"Are you going to stand there all night?" Flip yawned and stretched. "I'm going to fall asleep right here."

I giggled, narrowing my thoughts to the four-inch-wide piece of wood below me. This time the takeoff for my double-back was strong. I rotated well and when my feet touched down, I knew I had it. Taking several little steps, I wobbled, but stayed on the beam. I'd finally made it.

"Good girl!" Flip pounded me on the back as I jumped down. "I knew it was almost there."

"I had to get it one of these days," I shouted, excited that I would be able to add the more difficult combination to my routine for the championship.

"Now let's get out of here! It's been a long day."

"Yes, sir!" I gave him my best military salute. I started to leave, but the whir of a vacuum cleaner caught my attention. I looked over and spotted the back of a dark-haired boy, cleaning the floor-exercise area at the other end of the gym. Even from this distance I noticed his biceps bulging under his yellow T-shirt. I hadn't seen him here before. This was a new addition to the gym that I'd definitely have to look into!

I ran up the steps to my locker on the balcony. Gathering up my stuff, I flicked off the lights and stood in the shadows watching him. I could still only see his back but I knew the rest of him just couldn't be disappointing. If we met, what would he think of me?

I reached up to touch my French braid, much of which had come undone. My sun-streaked blond hair was okay, but I'd trade it any day for thick, dark curls like my best friend, Michelle's. I'm also only five feet tall—an advantage for a gymnast—but I feel like a pygmy next to everybody else, especially guys.

The sound of the vacuum echoed in the empty gym. "Hurry up, Kristy!" Flip yelled above the noise. "Your dad's waiting for you!"

Reluctantly, I tore my eyes away from the boy and went downstairs. But before I went outside, I had to take one last look over my shoulder.

When I got home, my mom called from the kitchen, "Michelle phoned—said to call her immediately." I took the stairs two at a time to reach my bedroom and flopped down on the patchwork bedspread that echoed the blue and white color scheme of the rest of my room. Dialing Michelle's number, I wondered what she would have to say tonight.

The phone rang twice before Michelle picked it up.

"Chelle, it's me. Sorry, but I stayed late."

Michelle squealed, "I thought you'd *never* call! Did you see him today?"

"Him? Who's him?" I tried to think of someone I should have seen. I could picture Michelle on the other end of the line, her dark eyes sparkling with excitement.

"Oh, Kristy, where have you been?" She sighed. "The new boy at school. He's *sooo* gorgeous."

There hadn't been any new boy in any of my classes, or I would have certainly noticed. "Don't keep me in suspense, tell me!"

"Well, turn to July on your *Men of USC* calendar," Michelle teased.

I thought about all those handsome pictures on the calendar. And I remembered July very well.

"*That* guy's at our school?"

"No, dummy! He just *looks* like him!"

I protested, "C'mon, Michelle, nobody in real life looks like that."

"Oh, but he does, honest!" she insisted. "Wait till you see him. You're going to drool."

"You bet I'll drool if he really does look like that," I said, giggling. "Does he have a name?"

Michelle's voice went soft and dreamy. "His name is Randy, Randy Harris, and he's perfect for you."

"Me?" I said. "What about you?" We had this way of deciding which of the boys at school were right for her and which were right for me. Unfortunately we were no closer to capturing them in reality than we were to snagging one of the calendar men.

"I need somebody tall and he's just average height," Michelle replied.

"Just how short is he?" I demanded.

There was a moment of silence while she thought about it. "Well, I think he's about five feet nine. But for you—"

"I know. Okay, I'll take him," I said, going along with the game.

6

She laughed. "Who knows, maybe you can get him to notice you, and there will be this zap of . . ."

"Hey, even if lightning flashed right in the middle of the school quad it wouldn't matter. I just don't have time for romance."

"But you *are* going to try to come to some of the dance tomorrow night, aren't you?" Michelle pleaded. "Won't Flip let you off an hour early?"

I hesitated. With a big meet coming up I was pretty sure there wouldn't be any way I could get out of workout early, especially since I wanted to include the new ending to my routine. But I also knew how disappointed Michelle would be if I couldn't make it.

"I'll try," I said weakly, "but you know Flip."

Michelle had also worked with Flip. It had been great having her on the team with me—until she grew six inches in one year. At five feet eight, she looked great in clothes, but her height pretty much knocked her out of gymnastics. Now she only helped me teach the little girls' Rainbow Team. She was my best friend, and she understood how I felt about gymnastics and my dream of becoming a member of the Olympic team.

7

"Kristy Warner, are you still there?"

I realized I hadn't been paying attention to what Michelle had just been saying. "Just tired, Chelle. Look, I'm starving. I really have to go."

"Please talk to Flip," she pleaded.

"Okay. See you tomorrow."

Just as I hung up the phone a little ball of white fur hit me from behind. I reached back and grabbed Bubbles, my Yorkshire terrier, and gave him a hug. "Come on. Let's go eat," I said.

"Kristy?" a small voice called from down the hall. I made a detour into my little sister's room and found her propped up against two pillows, the night-light casting a glow across her sleepy face.

"I tried to stay awake till you got home." She pulled one of her blond braids out from under her quilt.

I sat down on the edge of her bed. "What's up, Twerp?"

Lori's china-blue eyes opened wide, and she spoke with seven-year-old enthusiasm. "At recess, my teacher had me show the class a back bend. I did it real good, the way you and Michelle taught me at Rainbow practice."

"Great! I bet they were impressed!"

8

Lori smiled. "They all clapped."

"I'm sure they did!" I tucked the covers around her and she yawned, the freckles dancing across her nose. I gave her a hug and turned out the night-light. Then I headed for the kitchen where Mom was dishing up my dinner.

She handed me a plate of fried chicken and vegetables. "Hungry?"

"Starving!" I answered, and smiled. A strand of Mom's short, ash-blond hair fell forward, and she brushed it back off her forehead. Tired blue eyes smiled back at me as she set down a glass of milk, and I wondered why I hadn't noticed her fatigue before.

I eagerly started on my dinner while she made herself a cup of coffee and joined me at the table.

"Good day at school?"

"Yeah, about the same." That was how our conversation started each evening. Mom always wanted to know about school. She worries about me missing out on things because I'm so involved in gymnastics. "Everybody's excited about the dance tomorrow."

"Is there any way you could go?" she asked quietly.

I tried to sound cheerful so she wouldn't

9

think I cared about it very much. "No way! Not with the Elite meet only a month away. How's business?" I asked, to change the subject. My mom had a small shop in town. Besides kitchen items, she sold pastries, and coffees and teas from around the world. She spent most of every day working there. She loved it, and the long hours didn't usually bother her. But tonight she seemed depressed.

She stretched and sighed. "It was very slow today. Usually Thursdays are bad, but we had practically no customers at all."

"I'm sorry, Mom," I said.

"Oh, it'll pick up again, I'm sure," she said, forcing cheerfulness. "What's the homework situation, honey?"

I grimaced, thinking of the math I still had to do tonight. "I'd better get started." Untangling Bubbles from under my feet, I reluctantly headed for my books. There was algebra to finish and my Spanish notes to look over for a quiz in the morning. It was always the same—a push to get everything done, and never enough time for hanging out with friends or just having fun.

It wasn't until bedtime that I had a chance to think about the dance again. Staring out my bedroom window, I couldn't see any stars or even the moon. A fog bank blotted out all trace of light. I thought about tomorrow and wished I could go to the dance. My disappointment briefly clouded my anticipation of meeting the new boy at school. Would I ever have time to have a boyfriend like everyone else?

Chapter Two

Even from a block away, I could see Michelle leaning against the wall of Seagate High. We always met outside and walked to our lockers together. I'd overslept that morning and had to run part of the way to school. Shifting my books, I waved.

"You're late!" she called.

Catching my breath, I answered, "Yeah, I know. My five minutes' extra sleep turned into twenty!"

"Well, come on," she said. "You *do* want to see him, don't you?"

"Him?" I couldn't resist teasing her. Of course, I knew who she was talking about. Anyone who looked like one of the guys on the *Men of USC* calendar had to be seen to be believed.

We went inside and started down the hall. Michelle's thick, dark curls bounced as we peeked into each homeroom, trying to appear casual while we searched for the new boy. I thought Michelle's willowy figure looked great in her new white denim miniskirt, and I noticed she'd applied extra eye shadow and lip gloss. Suddenly I wished I had taken the time to do more than run a comb through my hair.

When we reached the end of the hall, we threw each other disappointed looks. "No luck, and the bell's going to ring any minute."

Michelle sighed. "He must be over in the other wing. I guess we'll have to wait until lunch."

Nodding, I rushed off to class, slipping into my seat just as the bell rang. I looked forward to algebra as much as I did to eye surgery. I had to keep a B average to stay in gymnastics, but this was one subject that simply didn't make any sense to me. The homework especially didn't make sense, and while I struggled with the last equation, the room grew suddenly quiet.

I looked up. The best-looking boy I'd ever seen was standing by Mr. Laird's desk, handing him some papers. Mr. Laird studied his paperwork and then told him to find an empty seat. I felt as though my heart had stopped beating. This just *had* to be Michelle's "calendar man"! I was staring so intensely that I'm sure I *willed* him to walk down my aisle and take the seat directly across from me.

He tossed his books on the desk and dropped into the seat. It was right then, at exactly 9:03, that he looked over at me and smiled.

"Hi," he said. "I'm Randy Harris."

I couldn't say a word. I just sat there, like a lump of clay, staring at him.

"Hey! Anybody home?"

That knocked me out of my trance, and I could feel a warm blush creeping up my face. How could I have acted like such a geek? "Hi, I'm Kristy Warner," finally came out. That was all the conversation we had time for before class began.

Before going over the homework, Mr. Laird introduced Randy to the class. I sneaked a quick look sideways and saw Randy looking back. Then he grinned and opened his algebra book.

The rest of the class was useless. I kept debating whether he really looked like the

July calendar man, and decided that Randy was much cuter. At some point between 9:03 and the end of class he glanced over at me again, and I looked into gray-blue eyes that reminded me of the ocean on an overcast day. His dark hair curled over his ears and was slightly windblown. Maybe he drove a convertible. I pictured him behind the wheel, and me beside him. Dreaming about driving along the moonlit beach, I didn't hear Mr. Laird call my name.

"Kristy, can you possibly wake up long enough to pass those papers up to the front?"

I gave a start and found Joe Murray, in the seat behind me, holding the homework papers over my shoulder. I had no idea how long he'd been waiting for me to take them. The whole class laughed. So did Randy. Flustered, I tried to regain my cool. Randy had to think I was a real jerk! I'd wanted to create an impression, and I had—class clod. When the bell rang I quickly loaded my books into my arms and fled from the room.

Lunchtime finally arrived and I grabbed an empty picnic table in the middle of the quad, spreading out my lunch to save a place for Michelle. As I looked at my ham sandwich, I didn't feel very hungry. Sharing my horrible

15

morning with Michelle seemed much more important than eating.

"Argh! What a terrible day!" Michelle let her books thud onto the table a few minutes later. "Old Corny gave us a pop quiz in history," she said, referring to her elderly, near-sighted world history teacher.

I moaned in sympathy. "Bad?"

"The worst! Who can remember all those dates? And who cares?" She ripped the plastic bag off a pita bread sandwich.

As she started eating, I said, "The new boy's in my algebra class."

Michelle almost choked on her sandwich. "No kidding! What did you think?"

"Gorgeous, absolutely gorgeous!" I pictured Randy's face with those startling gray-blue eyes. Then, recalling what a fool I'd made of myself, I realized there was little chance of those beautiful eyes ever smiling at me again. I sighed. "Oh, Michelle, I acted like a number-one jerk today."

"So tell me!"

"Well, first, I couldn't seem to get anything to come out when he said hi. I just sat there looking like I had a mouthful of peanut butter or something. Then I started daydreaming about riding around with him in his convertible . . ."

"He's got a *convertible*?" Michelle squealed.

I shoved my untouched lunch away. "No. I mean, I don't know."

When I finished telling her about my humiliation, Michelle draped her arm around my shoulders. "Don't worry. You'll knock him dead tomorrow."

"That's easy for you to say." I thought about how tongue-tied I had been, and cringed.

"Aren't you going to eat anything?" Michelle asked.

I shook my head and stuffed everything back into the paper bag. "I'm not hungry. I'll eat it later at the gym."

"Then let's go walk around," Michelle suggested.

We wandered around the quad, checking out the groups of students at tables in the middle and the couples under the trees.

"Hey, Kristy!"

I turned to see Joe Murray waving at me. He left two friends and walked over to us, grinning. "You get caught up on your sleep yet?" His reference to algebra class made me grimace and I struggled to keep that embarrassing blush from once again creeping over my cheeks. Meanwhile, I could see that his good looks and curly, blond hair impressed Michelle.

"I was just catching up on a few winks," I joked. I didn't want him to know how upset I'd been or he'd probably tease me for the rest of the year.

Michelle nudged me in the back, and I realized she didn't know Joe. "Joe, this is my friend Michelle."

"Hi, Michelle," Joe said. He seemed to notice her for the first time, and it was obvious that he liked what he saw.

One of Joe's friends called and he turned to go. "Try to stay awake!" he advised me, laughing.

I laughed too. "I'll give it my best shot."

Michelle watched as Joe joined his friends and walked off toward the parking lot. "Where have you been hiding him?" she asked.

"Joe? He's in a couple of my classes," I said, staring at her. Could Michelle really be interested in Joe Murray? I'd never thought of him as a possible romantic interest. But now I could see how he might appeal to Michelle. . . .

After school I walked to the gym. The American Gym Club was in one of a number of beige stucco buildings that housed small businesses. For four years, ever since Flip left the National Club downtown to start his own gym, I'd walked to that gym every afternoon after my fifth-period class.

Usually I looked forward to my practice sessions, but today everything had gone wrong. I still felt rotten about my meeting with Randy that morning, and now I felt really miserable about missing the dance tonight, knowing he might be there.

I hadn't minded missing school activities so much when Michelle was working out at the gym with me. There hadn't been as much pressure then. My determination to become an Elite gymnast was still there, but some of the excitement had gone. In the past, being in the select group of national-level gymnasts and competing against the best in the country was all I'd ever wanted. Why didn't I feel that way now?

I pulled open the locker-room door. Why did it always smell like dirty socks? I took off my street clothes and, opening my own locker, threw my clothes inside and pulled on a red-striped leotard. I had to stop agonizing over Randy and the dance, or I would never have the concentration I needed for the workout.

"Hey, Kristy! You mad or something?"

I looked up to see my teammate, Angelique,

watching me anxiously. Her cap of reddish-blond hair curled naturally around her face. Standing on the bench that ran in front of the lockers, her tiny frame towered over me, though we were about the same size.

I tried to smile. "Hi, Angel. Do I look that bad?"

"The scowl on your face would scare Godzilla! What's wrong?"

"Just thinking about the dance at school. Michelle really wants me to come, and for the first time I really want to go."

She thought for a minute. "But a chance to make it to Elite class and someday even have a shot at the Olympics is worth the sacrifice."

I brightened at the thought of the Olympics. Was it too much to hope that someday I'd be part of the team from the USA? If I could take it one step at a time, I just might get there. It was the dream of every gymnast, and I wasn't ready to give up that dream just yet. "Come on," I said to Angel. "Let's go warm up!"

Talking to Angel had cheered me up, and I headed over to the uneven bars. Working on the bars always exhilarated me. I loved the feeling of flying around in large loops, moving back and forth between the two levels in intricate maneuvers. I rubbed chalk on my hands. The calluses that covered my palms felt hard and brittle—not great hands for holding. A momentary vision of walking hand in hand with Randy flashed through my mind, and I felt another pang at having to miss the dance. *Forget it!* I told myself sternly. I needed all the concentration I could muster for my difficult bar routine.

My thoughts were completely taken up with gymnastics for the rest of the workout. It wasn't until I stood waiting for my dad to pick me up that I thought of the dance again. By now everyone would be dancing to the music of Cats and Cads, a local rock group. I closed my eyes and pictured my friends having a good time. Who would be dancing with Randy tonight? If I were there, would it have been me?

Chapter Three

The crisp fall air was making my nose tingle by the time Lori and I reached Michelle's front porch Saturday morning. We always picked Michelle up on our way to Rainbow Team practice. Michelle's mom let us in and told us that she was in the kitchen.

Lori settled herself on the floor with Michelle's Siamese cat and I pulled out a chair and sat down. "Now look who's late."

"I know. Why can't we teach this class on Saturday *afternoon*?" Michelle moaned. "Whoever chose this hideous time of the morning?"

I looked up at the clock above the stove: 8:45. "Seems to me I remember something about not wanting to break up the whole day so you and I can hit the beach in the afternoon."

"Okay, okay. Let's go before I decide to dive back into bed." Michelle dumped her dishes in the sink and grabbed her gym bag from the floor in the hall.

I tugged at one of Lori's braids. "Time to go."

As we walked along, I wondered why Michelle didn't bring up the subject of last night's dance. She was silent, walking along beside me. "Hey, what are you waiting for?" I finally burst out. "I thought you'd be dying to tell me all about the dance."

She glanced at me. "I thought maybe you wouldn't want to hear about it since you couldn't go."

"Come on, Michelle. Since when haven't I wanted to hear every juicy detail?"

She stopped right there on the sidewalk. "Oh, Kristy, I really am dying to tell you! I just didn't want to make you feel bad."

It felt good knowing she cared so much about me. She had sensed that I wasn't as casual about missing the dance as I let on. It was great having such a good friend.

"The music was terrific. The Cats played everything on the charts and anything we

23

requested and everybody was there. . . ." She broke off.

"Go on, get down to the good stuff. Who'd you dance with?" I thought I saw a trace of pink in her cheeks as she answered me.

"You'll never guess."

"Well, don't keep me in suspense."

She smiled, more to herself than to me. "I ran into Joe Murray. . . ."

"Joe!" I squealed. "Did he dance with you?"

"Yeah, well, we danced quite a few times."

I really felt excited for her. It had never crossed my mind to introduce her to him earlier. I had assumed that they knew each other. "That's great! Did he ask you out?"

"No," she said. "But he said he'd see me Monday."

"What else happened?" I urged.

Michelle thought for a minute. "Angel came in for a few minutes in the end. I looked for you—I thought you might have come with her."

"I never thought of it," I said. "I guess I thought it would be too late."

"Well, come next time, okay?"

"Okay." I wondered if she would ever mention Randy, and then I decided to come right out and ask. "Was the new boy there?"

She looked at me and raised an eyebrow. "Interested in Randy, are you?"

"I was just curious," I said, trying to sound nonchalant.

"Curious, huh? Sounds like more than that to me."

I made a face and admitted, "Well, maybe a little more than curious."

"He was there, and I kept track of everyone he danced with because I knew you'd ask."

"He danced with everybody?" I said sadly.

"Only the girls," Michelle joked. "But he didn't pick out anyone special."

I was glad to hear that, anyway. For a moment I wondered if he'd looked for me. But I would be the *last* person he'd be looking for, I decided, remembering our encounter in algebra class.

We reached the gym five minutes before our Rainbow Team was to start practicing. The Rainbows waited for us at the far end of the gym and Lori hurried to join them. Each of the seven-year-old girls wore a leotard in different pastels, together creating a cheerful splash of color. The rainbow patch sewn in the center of each leotard, below the scoop neckline, designated them as members of the team. Flip had formed this special group because of their exceptional abilities at a young age.

I pulled out the mini-trampolines for the girls and we started the workout with dive rolls over one of the padded blocks. The rest of the morning flew by and before I knew it, practice was over. "Okay, you can all go . . ." I stopped in midsentence as I looked up to see a young man getting the vacuum cleaner out of the cupboard. As he came toward me my mouth dropped open and I stood staring, oblivious to the little girls and Michelle. "Randy!" I whispered.

A lazy smile stole over his face as he recognized me, but he remained standing at the edge of the floor-exercise mats, leaning on the vacuum.

Michelle must have spoken to me four times before she shattered my trance. "Should I let the kids go?"

I glanced quickly at the clock and nodded. When I saw her big grin, I came out of my frozen state and walked toward Randy. "What are you doing here?" I asked as casually as I could.

"Sweeping," he answered, still smiling at me.

He must be the one I saw here Thursday night! I thought. I looked down at his plaid

26

Bermuda shorts that showed off muscular legs. When I looked back up my face flamed.

"You weren't at the dance." It was a statement, not a question, and I shivered—he had noticed!

"I—I had to come to workout," I mumbled, finally finding my voice. Why did I always get so tongue-tied around him?

"You're here a lot," he said.

I nodded. "So are you, it seems."

"I needed a part-time job, and they needed someone to vacuum three times a week, so here I am." His smile broadened. "Do I need a note from home?"

I relaxed a little and smiled too, brushing a lock of hair out of my eyes.

"What did you do to your hand?" Randy asked.

I looked down and realized that my callused palm must look painful to someone who didn't know. "Hazards of the bars." I tried to sound like it was nothing, but I hated having him see my ugly hands.

"It looks sore," he said, reaching out and taking my hand gently. My first thought was to pull away, but when a tingling sensation shot through me at his touch, I felt like holding on forever.

"It isn't. It doesn't hurt at all," I murmured.

"Well, I gotta get to work," he said, and moved away to plug in the vacuum cleaner.

"Do you like that boy?" I felt a tug at my leotard and looked down into Lori's upturned face.

Smiling, I put my finger to my lips. "Yes, but don't tell anyone. Can you keep a secret?" Lori's eyes opened wide and she nodded.

"Kristy!" Michelle called from the locker room. "Let's go! We're wasting sun!"

How true, I thought. These late-September days were still warm enough for the beach, but it did begin to get cool after three o'clock.

"Coming!" I called back. "Come on, Twerp. Let's get out of here."

I went into the locker room to change while Michelle waited for me. "What did you and Randy talk about?" she asked, her eyes twinkling. "Cute guy, huh?"

I hugged myself. "And how! I can't believe he works here."

"It'll give you a chance to get to know him better. And maybe even show off a little."

Thinking of the dumb way I'd acted the first time we met, I wondered if he would want to get to know *me* any better. But I hadn't been quite so dopey today.

I slung my bag over my shoulder. "Let's roll!"

As we reached the door, I couldn't resist taking one last look at Randy as he pushed the vacuum around the gym equipment. He was the boy I had always dreamed of—but somehow I'd never imagined my knight in shining armor would be pushing a vacuum cleaner!

Chapter Four

I promised to meet Michelle in twenty minutes so I raced home with Lori to gather up my beach gear. My turquoise beach towel still hung on the patio hook from last weekend. I rolled it around my sun oil and glasses before stuffing everything into my plastic beach bag.

In my room, I pulled out a red print bikini, untying the laces at the side so it didn't seem so brief in case Mom or Dad saw me on the way out. They didn't understand that this suit had twice as much fabric as those worn by most of the other girls at the beach. I pulled on a cutoff sweatshirt and changed my sneakers for sandals before heading back to the kitchen.

I tugged down the bottom of my suit when I saw Mom at the refrigerator getting out cold cuts for sandwiches. "Hi, Mom—I didn't know you'd be coming home for lunch."

She jumped a little at my voice. "Oh, Kristy, you startled me! It's slow at the store again so I left Sara in charge," she said, referring to the woman who worked part-time in her shop. "The beach again?"

"Yeah, not too many days left. I just want to fix a tuna sandwich." Quickly I made my sandwich and dashed off to meet Michelle.

To save time Michelle and I had decided to ride the bus to the beach and walk home. After we got off at our stop, we waited for traffic to clear before crossing Pacific Coast Highway to the section of beach where the kids from Seagate High hung out. In the fall the beach wasn't very crowded—fewer people came there from the inland towns. There were mostly regulars and locals now, but even in the middle of summer our crowd always found their special place.

I kicked off my shoes. It felt good to walk in the sand when it didn't burn your feet the way it did in July and August. We spread out our towels and I tightened the drawstrings on the sides of my bikini now that I was well out of Mom's sight. Then I pulled out the number-fifteen sunscreen she always made me bring.

"Will you do my back?" Michelle asked, handing me her bottle of suntan oil.

Rubbing the oil across her already brown skin, I felt sorry that the beach season was almost over. I handed her the bottle and sat down in front of her so she could do my back. "Anything you forgot to tell me about the dance?" I asked.

"About the dance, or about anyone in particular?" she teased.

"Yeah, especially about *him*." A sheepish grin stole over my face. "But about the others too."

Michelle stretched out on her towel, crossing one arm over her face to shield her eyes. "Well, Alison Baldwin showed up in another outrageous outfit and flirted with all the guys. She thinks she's so cool!"

"Nothing new." I pictured the petite sophomore who pranced around school as if she owned it and all the boys. "Did she dance with Randy?"

"A couple of times. No big deal. It makes

me sick the way she falls all over the boys and gives them that honey-voice treatment!"

"Aha!" I poked her in the ribs. "She must have latched onto Joe last night."

Scowling, Michelle propped herself up on her elbows. "It was sickening. And the worst part was that he seemed to enjoy it."

"Don't worry. I don't think any of the guys take her seriously." I waved to a couple of friends by the water and flopped down on my towel.

Michelle sat up and yawned. Then she nodded toward the shore. "Maybe it's time for a swim."

I didn't answer. I was watching a group of surfers who'd just come out of the water, laughing and talking. A few other kids walked over to join them. But all my attention suddenly focused on one dark-haired surfer— Randy Harris! He shook the water out of his hair and grinned as one of the other boys slapped him on the back.

Michelle saw him too. "That's Joe with them," she said. "Let's go over there, okay?" When I didn't say anything, she continued, "Please, Kristy, come with me."

I wanted to join the group as badly as she did, but I suddenly felt shy. Michelle tried again. "Come on. It's a great chance for us."

I brushed off the sand and straightened my bikini top. "What'll we do, just walk right up to them?"

"We'll act like we're going to take a swim and just *happen* to notice them," Michelle said.

So we walked down to the edge of the water and then slowly made our way over to the boys, who had already attracted a bunch of kids from school.

"Wow, were those waves great today!"

"I really wiped out on the last one."

"That one you guys caught to the left of the pier was super."

The conversation centered completely on the quality of the waves. Alison and some of her crowd of girls began to get restless, but I couldn't tear my eyes away from Randy.

Joe threw an arm around Randy's shoulders. "We got another one for the school surfing team," he told the others. "He's a natural."

Now Alison looked up at Randy. "I *love* surfers," she gushed.

That made me furious. I hoped no one noticed me glaring at her, but Michelle did. She poked me and I forced a smile. After all, I didn't own Randy. I hardly even knew him.

Joe looked over at Michelle. "Hi, Michelle! Did you see my last run?"

"No, I was working on my tan," she answered, gazing way too mushily at him, I thought. "But I'm sure it was wonderful."

Randy grinned at me. He didn't say a word, just stood there watching me, and I started getting embarrassed. I hoped my summer's accumulation of tan would hide my blush.

Michelle moved over beside Joe and they began laughing and talking together. I knew I had to do something, not just stand there staring at Randy like an idiot. I had almost worked up my courage to go talk to him when Greg Barnes, a basketball player, yelled, "C'mon, you guys! Let's have a game of volleyball." Then he beckoned to me. "I need you on my team, Half Pint."

I gritted my teeth. Why did he have to keep calling me that? I didn't want Randy to think of me as a kid. "No way, Greg. You'd just hog the ball!"

Joe headed over to the volleyball net and Michelle tagged along behind, motioning for me to follow her. I did, trying to resist looking over my shoulder to see if Randy was coming too. He did join us and as we divided into teams, I managed to get on his side.

The game was a lively one. Our team spent most of the time trying to keep the ball away from Greg, who had a deadly spike shot. We had all grown up playing volleyball in the sand and we loved the good-natured competition. The game ended with Greg spiking over the last two points to win. Our side demanded a rematch later.

"Hey, Half Pint," Greg called, "how about doing some back flips for us?" To people who weren't gymnasts flips always seemed impressive, and I jumped at the chance to show off a little for Randy. As I flipped across the sand, I heard my friends shouting.

"Atta girl!"

"Way to go!"

When my performance was over, I brushed the sand off my hands and joined Michelle.

"Flip would kill you," a disapproving voice said behind me, and I turned to see Angel standing there, her red curls wet with salt water.

I grinned. "What he doesn't know won't hurt him."

"Yeah, but it could hurt *you.* You step the wrong way in the sand and pull a muscle and you're done for the trials next month."

"Guess you're right," I admitted. I knew how important it was to be in good shape for the Elite gymnastic meets. There were a lot of girls trying out for that level, and Flip thought I had a good chance. But it was hard to focus on that now when I was having so much fun.

Angel gave me a quick wave. "Gotta go. I'm meeting Heidi at Jack-in-the-Box. But remember what I said." I watched her hurry off to join one of the other girls from the gym.

"Want to play Frisbee?" Michelle called as she and Joe headed for an open spot on the beach.

I shook my head. Suddenly I heard Randy's voice behind me. "Those flips looked really difficult."

This is what I had wanted—a chance to talk to him alone. I turned to face him. "Actually, they're easy. I learned how to do them when I was eight."

"Eight! You've been at this a long time!"

Smiling up at Randy, I noticed how thick the lashes were that framed those wonderful gray-blue eyes. When he grinned, a dimple showed in his cheek. Forcing myself to stop looking at him so hard, I answered, "Half my life."

"Want to go for a walk?" he asked, and I fell into step beside him as we headed to the water's edge. We walked for a while without talking, but it didn't feel uncomfortable at all. It felt friendly and nice.

Randy finally broke the silence. "I sure love living this close to the beach. There's something about the ocean. . . ."

"I know how you feel. Whenever I need to think about something I come down here." I sat down on the sand, looking out over the water.

"Me too," he agreed, sitting beside me. "Only I like to do it on a surfboard way out from shore."

We sat quietly for a few minutes until I changed the subject. "You sure know a lot of people for someone who just moved here."

"It kind of happened out there." He pointed out to the water where a few surfers paddled in a group. "I went out alone, but it didn't take long to meet everybody."

"Our surfing team is a great group of guys."

Randy nodded. "I noticed they weren't the usual bunch of flakes. Surfing's important to me, but not at the expense of school and everything else."

I smiled at him. "Joe says you're good."

"They want me to be on the team." A look of satisfaction crossed his face.

"Hey, that's great!" In my enthusiasm I

reached over and touched his arm. Then, realizing what I had done, I let go and grinned sheepishly, turning back toward the ocean.

Randy picked up a pebble and tossed it at the water. "The surfing team is really why I moved here to live with my sister."

I looked up in surprise. "Where's your family?"

"My dad's working in London for two years, but I didn't want to go. I've been living with my grandmother in Pasadena since my parents left last spring," he explained.

"Aren't you lonesome?" I knew I would be miserable living away from my family.

He shook his head. "I was at first, but now that I moved in with Julie—that's my sister— things are better. Plus, I'm back near the water. I hated living inland."

"Oh, I would too!" I agreed. I couldn't imagine living away from the beach.

"The water's like a magnet—especially the waves." He turned to look at me, and my stomach started a whole series of back flips all on its own. "I don't know how to describe it exactly, but you sit out there waiting for the big wave, one you can talk about for weeks. Then riding on it is a thrill you can't get anywhere else." He shook his head and jumped to his feet. "Wow, I didn't mean to go on like this." I thought I saw a little blush on his face right before he turned away.

We didn't say much as we walked back up the beach, but I felt something special between us, and I thought that he felt it too. I knew he wouldn't be a stranger when I saw him in algebra on Monday.

Chapter Five

Seagate High was buzzing on Monday after they announced the auditions for *Annie*, the school musical. This was an important event every year, and from the noise in the halls, it seemed everyone in the school looked forward to trying out. Everyone except me. I just didn't have time for things like that as well as gymnastics. I found myself wondering what it would be like to be in the show, and I was soon lost in wistful dreams of stage sets, stage makeup, and bright spotlights.

Michelle caught up with me before algebra class. "Kristy!" she cried. "Did you hear the announcement? They're doing *Annie*! I'm so excited! I can't wait to try out!" She caught her breath. "Do you think I'll get a part?"

I tried to scrape up some enthusiasm. "Yeah, I heard. I'm sure you'll get a part, Chelle." Michelle would probably be a good actress, and she needed something to replace the gymnastics that she no longer shared with me.

Michelle grinned as if I'd just told her she had the lead in the show. "Thanks, Kristy. I wish you had time to try out too! We'd have so much fun! Gotta run now." She waved back at me as she dashed off toward her history class.

I walked into algebra class and slammed my books on my desk, feeling blue. I would never be able to be in a school play, not with all the time I had to spend at the gym. Dropping into my chair I muttered half aloud, "Cut it out, Kristy. You're already doing what you want."

"You're doing what?"

I glanced up to see Randy sliding into his desk across from mine. "Oh, nothing. Just feeling sorry for myself, I guess."

"Well, you look pretty glum considering that the rest of the kids are acting like the school's closing for an extra vacation. You did hear about the show, didn't you?"

Forcing a smile, I nodded. "I know—that's

my problem. It's hard to get excited about something terrific when you know you can't be part of it."

"Because of gymnastics, huh?" he asked sympathetically.

I nodded, noticing the way his dark hair was combed back on the sides, but still curled around the tops of his ears. No wonder he attracted all the girls.

The room filled with students noisily discussing the play, and I leaned across the aisle so we could still hear each other. "Really, I *do* like gymnastics. It's just that sometimes I wish I could be two people."

"You're hardly big enough to be one person, let alone two," he teased.

I laughed. "What's size got to do with it?" As I gave Randy an exaggerated shrug, my elbow caught my purse and sent it flying off the desk, spilling the contents onto the floor.

"Oh, no!" I moaned, watching all my junk roll under Randy's seat and down the aisle. I leaned over and started grabbing everything I could reach, stuffing it quickly into my purse. Looking up, I saw Randy examining a handful of makeup he had picked up. His gray-blue eyes twinkled as he arched an eyebrow.

"Purple?"

I snatched a clear plastic case of eye shadow out of his hand and reached for the other things, but he held them out of my reach.

"Give them to me, please," I said through tight lips, aware that we had attracted the attention of the rest of the class. From the sound of smothered giggles I knew everyone but me thought it was extremely funny.

Randy read the label on one of my lip glosses. "Kissing Potion?" He looked at me in mock amazement. "Does it work?"

Everybody broke up laughing. I wished I could vanish in a cloud of smoke. I started to pick up my books to run out of the room, but at that moment Mr. Laird came through the door.

"Class! What's going on here?" the teacher bellowed above the commotion.

Quickly the laughter died and I stared at my desk to avoid seeing any leftover grins.

I felt a warm hand nudge my arm and heard Randy whisper, "I'm sorry," as he put my eyeliner pencil and two lip glosses on my desk. I couldn't say anything—I knew if I tried I would burst into tears.

Somehow I got through the class, but when the bell rang I grabbed my books and scooted out of the room before anyone, particularly Randy, could say anything to me.

By lunchtime I had calmed down enough to see a little humor in the situation while I told Michelle about the incident. If it had happened to someone else, I probably would have thought it was really funny too.

"Oh, well, guys only tease girls they like," Michelle said when I had finished, trying to control the grin threatening to take over her face.

I groaned. "You sound just like my mother!"

"You'll have to admit, Randy knows who you are now."

"He sure does." I shuddered at the impression I had made on him. "The class jerk!"

Michelle concentrated on her sandwich, and I thought about the way Randy had sounded when he whispered "I'm sorry." He hadn't been teasing then, I was sure of it. Looking around the quad, I searched for him, finally locating him with the members of the surfing team, lounging under a shady acacia tree. As our eyes met I realized he had been watching me look for him. He had a funny expression on his face, almost a smile, but mingled with a look of confusion.

Tearing my eyes away from his, I looked down at my crumpled lunch bag and popped my last carrot stick into my mouth, not wanting to talk to him right now. I just couldn't trust my feelings. I knew I should be angry at him, but if he was genuinely sorry . . .

To avoid speaking to Randy, I kept Michelle sitting at the table discussing the play until it was time to go to class.

We did a lot of reading in history, and then our teacher gave us time to start on our homework so the hour passed quickly. As soon as class was over, I hurried to my locker, glad that as far as I was concerned, school was over for the day. I was on my way to the gym for practice, which took the place of PE in my school schedule, and I hoped the exercise would help me work out my frustrations. Since the other kids were still in class, the school grounds were empty when I went outside.

"Kristy!" I heard Randy calling my name.

Surprised, I turned to face him as he ran over to me.

"You off to the gym?" he asked, and when I nodded, he continued, "Do you mind if I walk with you part of the way?"

"You don't have a class?"

He fell into step beside me. "Only drama,

46

and we're working alone on monologues. I think I've got mine down. I'll get back before anyone notices I'm gone."

We walked along side by side, the air practically crackling with the silence. Having no idea what to say, I just kept quiet. I sure didn't want to sound stupid!

Finally, Randy said hesitantly, "I'm sorry about this morning. I didn't mean to embarrass you, honest."

"That's okay," I said, though I didn't really think it was okay at all. Staring down at the sidewalk, I studied cracks I had never noticed before.

He went on, "I was just teasing, but I guess it didn't come across that way."

I didn't know what to say so I just looked up and smiled at Randy.

"Still friends then?"

"Sure," I said with a shrug. "You'd better get back before Mrs. Hill calls on you."

He stopped and grinned. "Thanks, Kristy! See ya later."

I watched Randy run back toward school, hoping he wouldn't get into trouble, and wondered what he meant by "friends." Was that all he wanted to be?

When I arrived at the gym, I changed my clothes and went over to where my team

47

worked out. It felt good to go through the warm-up exercises, and for a while I forgot about Randy, the school play, and all the other activities that I missed. Angel waved me over to the mats to help her with handstand push-ups.

"I heard you went to the dance," I said, holding onto her feet.

"I guess . . . you got me . . . interested." She spoke in little spurts as she continued with the exercise. "I . . . went by the school . . . on my way home . . . stopped in . . . for a few minutes."

Letting her feet down to the mat when she was finished, I said wistfully, "Wish I'd gone too."

"Hey! Next time we'll catch the last hour together."

"Yeah," I agreed as we headed over to the vault. We usually worked an hour on each event and then finished on whatever we chose.

But from then on the workout was a disaster. This just wasn't my day. First the play, then my humiliation in algebra, and now I kept falling off the balance beam.

"What's wrong, Kristy?" Flip asked at last. Looking up, I shrugged. "I'm just kind of down today."

48

"Anything important?"

I smiled a little, knowing that Flip was always on the alert for anything that might affect the performance of his gymnasts. "Just a couple of things at school. . . ."

"Is that all!" he said, relieved.

I turned away. The gym was all that mattered to Flip, and he assumed we all shared the same enthusiasm. And until now, I always had. Gymnastics had been my whole life. But now I was beginning to wonder if that was enough.

Chapter Six

As Dad drove me home from the gym, I pushed my seat back and closed my eyes, agonizing over whether I could share my mixed feelings about gymnastics with my parents. Dad was so proud of all my accomplishments and he also dreamed of seeing me become an Elite gymnast.

"Here we are!" Dad pulled the car into our driveway, then glanced over at me. He ran his hand through his graying brown hair and frowned. "Are you okay, honey?"

"Sure," I responded automatically, realizing that there was no way I could tell him my doubts.

He flipped off the lights and sat looking at me. "You seem a little tense tonight."

I smiled at him. "Just tired." I leaned over and hauled my backpack out of the backseat.

In the house, Dad went into the family room while I tossed my backpack on the hall table and walked into the kitchen. Mom was sitting at the table with her head resting on her folded arms. When she heard me, she looked up and managed a weak smile, but she didn't look happy.

"Something wrong, Mom?" She looked so depressed, and in my mood I'd been hoping for a little sympathy!

"It's just everything piling up." She got up and went to the microwave for my dinner—she and Dad had already eaten. "I've been worrying about the shop . . . it's just not doing very well these days." She sighed as she set the plate in front of me, then sat down across from me. I noticed a lot of tiny lines around her eyes. Had they always been there, I wondered, or was this something new?

"What's wrong with the shop?" I asked.

She sighed again. "The shop itself is fine. There just aren't many customers."

"What happened to all the people who usually come in? You've always had lots of customers before."

"They're all going to the new mall near the freeway," she said. "The whole downtown area is having trouble."

I reached out and took her hand, wishing I could think of some way to help, but I didn't have any ideas. This was definitely not the time to share my problems with her. I would just have to come to a decision about gymnastics without any help from either of my parents.

After rinsing my dishes and stacking them in the dishwasher, I went up to my room to do my homework. Fortunately there wasn't much tonight, and it didn't take me very long.

When I finished my English assignment, I got up to stretch. Throwing myself across the bed, I buried my face in the pillow and started thinking about Mom again. Though Dad had a good job managing a grocery store in Huntington Beach, I knew my parents counted on the profits from her shop to help pay for my and Lori's gymnastic expenses. It wasn't fair for me to use up so much of the family's extra money. Even when Mom's shop was doing well, she and Dad went without things to pay the gym bills. What was I going to do now? I couldn't keep taking money from them when the shop wasn't making a profit, especially when I wasn't sure I wanted to continue with gymnastics anyway.

I didn't know what to do. I heard the door squeak open and Bubbles came in and jumped up on the bed beside me. He whimpered a little and nuzzled me, getting as close as possible. His almost-black eyes looked awfully sad, as though he could feel my confusion and sorrow. It felt good to have someone care—even a dog.

"Oh, Bubbles," I groaned, "what am I going to do about the gym . . . and Mom's shop . . . and the money?"

Pushing Bubbles off my stomach, I reached for the phone to call Michelle. But after dialing her number, I hung up before it could ring. Michelle couldn't make up my mind for me—I had to do it on my own.

Suddenly, an idea came to me—I would get a job! If I could work Saturday afternoons and Sundays, maybe I could earn enough to keep me at the gym until I knew for sure if I wanted to quit. Why hadn't I thought of that before? Tomorrow I would ask Michelle to help me decide where to look for work. Feeling a little better, I kicked off my sneakers and pulled the covers over me, leotard and all.

On my way to algebra class on Monday, I saw Randy standing by the classroom door. Could he possibly be waiting for me? A smile lit up his face when he caught sight of me, and I quickly looked in my notebook to find the list I'd made of things to talk to him about. I hadn't gotten a very good start—only two things:

1. Surfing
2. Play tryouts

Closing the notebook, I joined him at the door. "Hi, Randy!"

"Hi. Uh—how did it go in gym the other day?"

"Uh—okay, I guess."

"Good. Uh—well . . ."

Randy didn't seem very comfortable talking to me, either. Obviously he hadn't made a list. I decided to jump right in with item number one. "How's surfing?"

He grinned. "Oh, it's great. I joined the team."

"Terrific!" I headed for my desk as other

kids started coming into the room, and Randy took the seat across from me.

He dropped his books on the desk. "I went to the beach early Sunday morning. The waves were great south of the pier—five to six feet."

I gave a low whistle. Those were good-sized waves, all right, and I knew without asking that there must have been a mob at the beach. Word travels like voodoo drums when the surf is up.

Since the conversation seemed to be slowing down, I decided it was time for number two on my list. But before I could speak, Randy brought the subject up himself. "I'm trying out for *Annie*."

That surprised me for some reason.

"You know, auditions are Friday night," he reminded me.

"Oh, yeah, right!" I said. "What part are you trying out for?"

Randy shrugged. "Just one of the small parts. I don't have much time with school, surfing, and my job at the gym."

I sighed. "I know all about that feeling."

Suddenly he said, "Hey! Why don't you come over to auditions on Friday night?"

He actually wanted me to come! My heart felt light as excitement bubbled up inside me. Now if only I could get there! Trying not to sound as eager as I felt, I said, "I'll really try to make it."

"Try hard," Randy said, smiling warmly at me. Then Mr. Laird called the class to attention, and I tried to focus on the lesson. But I couldn't help thinking about Randy's invitation to the auditions. It wasn't exactly a date, but he *had* invited me, and I would look forward to it all week.

My gymnastics practice improved over the next few days. Flip had scheduled an extra meet so my new combination could be tried out in competition before the Elite meet. I was excited about that, and I knew I couldn't let Flip down until I was sure in my own mind whether I was going to quit or not.

But I was still anxious to find a job. Since we would only be doing optional routines, the meet would be finished on Saturday, which meant I'd be able to start working on Sunday. But who would ever hire me, considering my limited hours? I scanned the Help Wanted ads in the paper, but I couldn't find anything that looked like a possibility.

Friday night, workout seemed to go on forever. When Flip finally dismissed us and I bolted for the shower in the locker room, it was five minutes to nine. I sure hoped they hadn't finished tryouts early!

Breaking all records for quick showers, I slipped into a light blue, crinkly, long-sleeved blouse and navy pants. As I came out of the locker room, Flip gave me an admiring whistle. "Well, well, aren't you looking great? Got a date?"

I laughed. "No—just going to play tryouts at school."

"Tryouts!" Flip stared at me in astonishment. "You're not trying out for a play? You don't have time for that!"

"Of course not," I explained quickly. "I'm just going to watch some friends."

He shrugged. "Well, okay. But don't stay out late."

"Okay, Mommy," I shouted over my shoulder as I slipped out the door.

I practically ran all the way to school, and I was relieved to see that the lights were on and the doors were open. But when I hurried into the hall, I didn't see any lights on in the theater and my stomach turned over. Had everybody gone home? Surely Randy would have waited for me. But I had only said I would *try* to get there—maybe he'd thought I wasn't coming at all. Then I heard clapping, and I opened the door to the auditorium. The stage was lit up, but the seating area was black. As my eyes adjusted to the darkness, I saw Mrs. Hill sitting in an aisle seat, holding her clipboard. I couldn't pick out Michelle or Randy from the rest of the kids in the audience.

I groped my way down the aisle and slid into a seat about halfway back.

"Attention!" Mrs. Hill called out. "Everyone auditioning for Miss Hannigan go backstage."

Now that my eyes had grown accustomed to the dark, I could make out Michelle's tall figure going behind the side curtain. After a heavyset girl in my English class read for the part, Michelle came onto the stage. She gave a great performance. It showed that she had spent a lot of time preparing—she didn't even have to use the script.

"Hi!" someone whispered, and Randy slid into the seat next to me. "When did you get here?"

"Just a few minutes ago," I whispered back. "Wasn't Michelle terrific?"

He nodded. "She ought to get the part. She was better than anybody else."

We watched the rest of the girls read, and then the boys began trying out for Daddy Warbucks. When Mrs. Hill announced the auditions for Miss Hannigan's brother,

Rooster, Randy went up onstage. I thought he read very well, and hoped he would get a part. It would be another good way for him to meet new people.

When the auditions were finally over, the overhead lights came on and Mrs. Hill thanked everyone for coming. I walked over to Michelle.

"You got here!" she squealed, giving me a big hug. "Did you see my audition? How'd I do?"

I grinned, and said in my most theatrical voice, "You were perfectly splendid, my dear. Tonight a star is born!"

Michelle giggled. "Oh, thanks, Kristy! I can't wait until they post the cast list." We began walking toward the door. "How are you getting home?"

As I started to speak, Randy came up beside me. "I was just going to ask Kristy if I could walk her home." He looked down at me. "Okay?"

I wanted to jump up and down, shouting, "Yes, yes!" but instead I smiled and agreed graciously, waving good-bye to a grinning Michelle.

The cool night air hit us as we walked out of the school and started down the street. I snuggled into my jacket, glad that I had remembered to bring it along. It was so warm during the day, I usually forgot.

"I'm glad you could come," Randy said.

"So am I," I answered. "I would never have thought of it if you hadn't mentioned it."

Randy laughed. "Lucky for me I did!"

I smiled up at him. "I hope you get the part."

"Me too," he agreed. "But no big deal if I don't. I'll just try out for the next show. I really like acting."

Then he reached out and took my hand, and I felt as if a hundred rubber balls were bouncing around inside my stomach. His hand felt so warm and protective around mine.

"You have cold hands," he said, taking both my hands in his and rubbing them. "Cold hands . . ."

"Warm heart," I finished, and we both laughed.

"I'm glad to know that about your heart," he said, and tried to stuff his left hand and my right into his jacket pocket. When they stuck halfway in, I got the giggles, and he yanked them free without letting go.

"I can't help it if you have such big hands," he joked, and began swinging our clasped hands back and forth, as if we were two little kids.

When we reached the traffic light at the corner, Randy let go of my hand to push the Walk button. I was glad when he took it again on the other side of the street. This time we walked along in silence. I wondered if he would try to kiss me when we got to my house. The crazy way he had been acting tonight, he might even kiss me right here on the street! I smiled to myself, kind of hoping he would.

We reached my house and went onto the porch. I wished Mom hadn't left the porch light on—we might as well have been on-stage.

"It was fun tonight," I said, turning to face him. "You were really awfully good." Was he going to kiss me now?

He reached out and took my other hand. "Thanks again for coming."

I didn't know whether to close my eyes or just stand there waiting for him to bend down and touch my lips with his.

"Maybe we can go out together sometime," he said.

"I'd like that." Was he going to go on talking forever?

He stood there smiling at me, the porch light gleaming on his dark hair. "Maybe you could come to a surf meet."

"I'll try." I could hardly breathe as we stood there looking at each other. Then my knees turned to jelly as his face moved closer to mine. This was it, the moment I had been waiting for!

And then he kissed the tip of my nose and bounded down the porch steps.

I stared after him until he reached the first streetlight and looked back to wave. Did that kiss mean as much to him as it did to me? I wondered. Did he realize I'd been expecting a *real* kiss?

Leaning against the door, I gazed up at the stars in the dark sky. I just knew that this was the beginning of something very special!

Chapter Seven

Monday morning Michelle was waiting for me in front of school wearing a sly grin. I knew something was up. "What took you so long?" she burst out when I got within hearing range. "I've been here forever!"

I pretended not to notice her excitement. "No reason to hurry—just another average Monday morning."

"Average! This is definitely *not* an average morning. I'm dying to tell you my super terrific news, and you're late."

"I'm listening," I said.

She gave me a smug smile. "Guess who called last night?"

"Your cousin from New York?" I suggested as seriously as I could manage.

"Cut it out, Kristy! This is special."

I decided to stop teasing her. "Sorry, Chelle. Tell me who called."

Michelle was positively glowing as she said, "Joe! Can you believe it? He finally called!"

I shared her excitement, knowing how wild I would be if Randy called me. "That's great! What did he say? Did he ask you out?"

"Sort of," she said as we started walking into the school.

"What do you mean, 'sort of'?"

"Well, he mentioned the movies next Friday night, but he didn't make it very definite."

I let out a loud whoop. "That sure sounds like a date to me! You'll probably see him today and find out the time."

"I hope so." Michelle sighed happily.

How lucky she was, I thought. If only Randy would ask me out—even though I probably couldn't go.

Michelle must have read my mind because she said, "It would be so neat if you and Randy could double with us."

"Oh, Chelle, you know how much I'd like that . . . but even if he asked me, I've got workout, and then there's the meet on Saturday. . . ." My voice trailed off and

Michelle didn't say anything, either. I'm sure she was dreaming about her date Friday night, and all I could look forward to was a gymnastic meet.

When we reached my locker, I decided to change the subject. "Michelle, I need to talk to you. Do you have any idea where I can get a job?"

"A job?" She stared at me in amazement. "How can you take a job? You don't have time!"

I sighed. "I know. But I really need to make some money."

"Give me time to think about it," she said at last. "When could you work?"

"Weekends," I answered, and then groaned when I remembered my other commitments. "At least, after Rainbows . . . but not next Saturday because of the meet."

Michelle ran her hand through her curls. "That's a tall order, but I'll check around."

"Thanks, Michelle!" I opened my locker, my thoughts turning to Randy. A blush crept across my face as I remembered Friday night. He must have known that I had expected him to kiss me. What if I had closed my eyes and he'd left me standing there?

As Michelle and I headed for our classes, we saw a group of students gathered around the bulletin board in the main hall where Mrs. Hill was trying to tack up an announcement.

"The auditions!" Michelle squealed. "I bet she's posting the cast list!" She ran over to join the crowd trying to read over Mrs. Hill's shoulder. A few shrieks came from the kids in front, but I couldn't see who had gotten parts. Michelle wormed her way into the mob, disappeared from view, then emerged from the other side waving frantically and shouting, "I got it! I got it! I got the part!" She grabbed me and whirled us both around, sending my books flying in all directions.

"Terrific!" I said. I started to pick them up. "I knew you had it. You were so good!"

"I can't believe it! I actually got the part of Miss Hannigan!" Michelle threw her lunch bag up in the air and caught it, then stopped dead. "Oh, there's Joe at his locker."

I gave her a playful shove. "Get going and go tell him—if he hasn't already heard you."

She grinned at me. "Okay. See you at lunch," she said, and hurried toward Joe's locker.

"Care for some books?"

Turning, I found myself face-to-face with Randy, who offered me the rest of the books I had dropped. Smiling, he said, "You seem to have forgotten these."

"Thanks, Randy." Remembering his audition, I asked, "How'd you do?"

"I got the part of Rooster," he said. "I just hope I can handle it with the job at the gym and the surf team."

"You'll be as busy as I am," I joked. "Anyway, I'm glad you got it."

"Me too. But with surfing practice three days a week, I'm going to be bushed." He stopped and took a deep breath. "Our first meet is a week from Saturday . . . I was wondering if maybe you'd like to come?"

Delighted, I asked, "What time?" My mind was already racing ahead, planning how I could get out of coaching the Rainbow Team just this once. Maybe Michelle could handle it.

"Starts at seven."

I groaned. "In the *morning*?"

"Yeah." He grinned at my reaction. "Think you could get up that early?"

"Oh, sure!"

The warning bell interrupted us and after saying good-bye, we went our separate ways. Even getting up at six sounded great. I wondered if the buses ran that early. Regardless, I knew I would be there to watch Randy's first surfing meet.

*　　*　　*

That night after I finished my dinner, Mom joined me at the table with her cup of tea. Once again I noticed how tired she looked. "How's it going, Mom?" I asked.

She shook her head. "Not good. I let Sara go today."

"Sara's gone?" Mom's assistant had been with her since she had opened the shop five years ago. I just couldn't believe it.

"She's going to travel with her husband." Mom stared down at her tea for a minute, then added, "If business picks up, she'll come back after their trip."

Somehow I felt that Mom didn't believe it would pick up. If only my gymnastics expenses weren't such a drain on our family finances. I decided it was time to tell her my plan. "By the way, Mom. I'm going to try and find a job to help with the gym bill."

"A job?" she repeated. "Oh, Kristy, no!"

I leaned across the table and took her hand. "Don't worry—I have it all figured out, the hours and everything."

"But you don't have time for a job. The gym is so demanding and you need to keep your grades up. . . ."

"They won't go down, I promise."

But none of my arguments seemed to make a difference. She kept telling me we would manage and I knew we would if the shop became successful again. Until then, I needed to do my part. It made me feel terrible to think that I wasn't holding up my end in the family. I decided I would find a job even if I had to do it secretly!

When I opened the gym door on Saturday morning, I was surprised to see so many kids there already. Usually I was one of the first to arrive. Warm-ups started two hours before a meet, but I guess everyone wanted to work extra hard, since this would be the last competition before the Elites.

"Hey, Kristy!" Angel shouted at me from the beam area. "You got your double ready for today?"

I nodded and pulled my coat closer over my red team leotard, hating to take it off in the cold gym. Today would be my first competition with my new combination on the beam, and I was scared to death. I could feel the tightness in my muscles and my palms felt clammy. The combination had to be included today—no chickening out. If it didn't go well this morning, it would have to be scratched from my routine for the Elite Trials next month.

I finished practicing all my events before

the spectators started to fill the bleachers. As I turned to join my team, I was surprised to see Randy making his way down a crowded aisle. Waving, he picked his way through gym bags and the children who were sitting on the floor along the edge of the mats.

"Hey! I'm glad you came!"

He grinned at me. "I saw a notice about this meet on the bulletin board—I've come to offer my services."

"You gonna chalk the bars for me?" I teased.

"I thought maybe I could get out the vacuum and clean around the other contestants—play games with their concentration," he joked.

Picturing him out there with his vacuum, calmly sweeping his way around the floor routines, I burst out laughing. "You're crazy!"

"Just trying to be helpful, ma'am."

"Here's hoping I won't need extra help."

We stood there looking at each other, not knowing what else to say. Finally he reached out to shake my hand. "Well, good luck."

I hoped he didn't notice how I trembled when I took his hand. "Thank you, kind sir!" I said. Then I ran off to join my teammates in Flip's office.

*   *   *

Later as I sat waiting for my turn on the beam, I sneaked a look into the stands and found Randy watching me—not the girls who were performing, but *me.* I smiled, hoping he knew it was for him. Now I really had to concentrate. I knew I would have to forget all about Randy to get that layout right.

Finally, the judge signaled me to begin. I saluted and mounted with a front somersault onto the beam. The first two thirds of my routine went smoothly as I executed each move as I had in meets for years. But as I approached the new combination, I started to feel tense. Knowing I had to be perfectly centered over the beam, I threw myself into the air and executed a back flip. Just before my feet came down, I sensed that I was a bit off balance. I had to get both feet on the beam first or I would lose an extra half point.

I landed hard. Not great, a little wobbly, but I had made it! I would lose that half point, but I knew the difficulty of the move would carry me through, and my score would show it. Soaring high on my double twisting dismount, a tremendous sense of satisfaction flooded through me. My doubts about continuing gymnastics seemed far away and I basked in the sweet moment of triumph. Maybe I didn't really want to quit after all.

The meet ended and we marched off to the music. At the end of the gym I saw Randy leaning against the bleachers watching me. As I made my way toward him, I felt as if I were floating.

"That's pretty impressive stuff," he said when I came up next to him.

"Thanks. I'm feeling pretty good about it myself now. It wasn't a sure thing," I confessed. I wished he would give me one of those big hugs that everyone else seemed to be giving the other gymnasts, but he didn't.

"I had no idea you were that good," Randy went on.

I felt myself blushing. "On the beam I'll only take second place. But I should do well in all-around."

He reached for my hands and squeezed them. "Hey, you're number one in my book!"

With my hands in his, I was speechless. I was so happy that I wanted to turn cartwheels all over the gym and shout at the top of my lungs, but I could only stand and stare at him.

He finally broke the silence. "I can't stay for the awards. I've already missed part of surfing practice."

I felt a pang of disappointment, but forced a smile. "Thanks so much for coming."

I don't know how long I stood there after he left, but Angel finally came to drag me off to the awards ceremony. As I stood on the blocks accepting my ribbons, one in each event, I felt numb. The real elation would come next month at the Elite Trials . . . *if* I made it. But I wasn't going to think about that now. Randy's words "You're number one in my book," along with the success of my new routine, had made this a day to remember.

Chapter Eight

Hanging by my knees from the parallel bars on Tuesday evening, I relaxed after a long workout. Looking up, I noticed Michelle sitting on the edge of the mat. When she caught my eye, she applauded.

"Fantastic!" she exclaimed. "Why didn't you tell me your routine looked so good?"

Laughing, I got down and collapsed beside her. "How could I know? I've never seen it myself."

Michelle grinned at me. "Don't you want to know what I'm doing here?"

"What's up?" I asked, sensing her excitement.

She gave me a wide smile. "Joe finally asked me out!"

"He did? When? Tonight? I thought you were at play practice."

Michelle patted my arm. "Slow down and I'll tell you."

"Okay, okay!"

"He stopped by the theater to see Randy—he said. But he ended up talking mainly to me."

"Did he come right out and ask you?" I prodded.

"I'm getting to that." She smiled. "Actually, he sort of slipped it in."

I gave Michelle a big hug. "Terrific! I was sure he would sooner or later. When's your date?"

"Seven-thirty Friday. I'm so excited! How will I ever get through the next three days?"

Trying to sound enthusiastic, I said, "Congratulations." I really was happy for Michelle, but I wished that Randy had asked me too. Thoughts about his coming to the meet last Saturday raised my spirits a little. And he *had* asked me to the surf meet. That was kind of a date.

". . . sort of hung around . . . Hey! Are you listening?"

I blinked and realized Michelle was still talking. "Sorry, Chelle. Just daydreaming, I guess."

"How can you drift off when I have so much more news?" she said, pouting.

"More news? Tell!"

She shrugged. "Well, you know the biggest dance of the year, the Snowflake Ball? I found out when it is! Alison and her airhead friends are on the decorating committee—it was easy to worm it out of her."

"Michelle!" I gave her a menacing look. *"When is it?"*

"Sorry—it's January seventeenth."

My heart sank. I felt like I had just swallowed a large rock. I'd secretly hoped that Randy might ask me to the dance, but even if he did, I couldn't possibly go. I would be out of town.

"Kristy, what's wrong?" Michelle asked, seeing my crestfallen expression.

I moaned, "Everything! That's the night before the second Elite Trial, and I'll be in Los Angeles."

Michelle thought about that for a minute, then brightened. "Don't worry. You'll qualify at the first one, and you won't have to go in January."

"Don't I wish!"

"You will. Now all we have to do is get Randy and Joe to ask us to the dance. Got any ideas how we pull that one off?" Unfortunately, I didn't have a clue. I couldn't even figure out a way to get Randy to ask me to the movies, let alone the biggest dance of the year!

Michelle got to her feet. "I've got to run. See you tomorrow morning, and think about it, okay?"

"Sure," I said. "Thanks for telling me all your news." Watching her leave the gym, I admired how well she had adjusted to being out of competitive gymnastics. She didn't seem to miss it at all. She was involved in so many activities . . . and now there was Joe. I wondered if I would do as well if I dropped gymnastics too.

After doing a few strength exercises I changed into street clothes, got my gym bag, and leaned against the outside door waiting for Dad. I was also waiting for Randy. If he came to vacuum, he would have to fall over me to get inside.

But Randy didn't show up. I slumped into the car after Dad honked.

"Good workout?" he asked.

"Yeah, it was okay," I mumbled.

He glanced over at me. "You don't sound exactly like a ball of fire."

"Just tired." "Tired" usually worked as an excuse when I was feeling low.

The one bright spot was Randy's surfing meet. I could hardly wait. But would he have any time to spend with me?

After a very early bus ride on Saturday morning, I found Randy and he led me to a blanket he had brought for me to sit on. It was such a thrill to watch him surf, cutting along the crest of the waves.

When he came out of the water, I hung back while he accepted compliments from the rest of the team. Then his eyes met mine and he gave me a special smile. My heart started pounding like crazy and my knees threatened to buckle as I walked over to him, so I reached out to steady myself by grabbing the school flag that was planted in the sand.

Randy's muscles rippled as he peeled down the top of his wet suit, pulled on a red sweatshirt, and took two cans of soda out of the cooler next to the blanket. As he handed me one, he said, "Want to walk out on the pier? We can watch the rest of the guys from there."

I nodded, glad he wanted to be with me.

There were few people on the pier this early. Only a solitary police car crept along toward the end. We stopped at a good place to see the action and leaned over the railing side by side. The cool wind blew back the hood of my sweatshirt and I didn't pull it up again. My hair would soon be in tangles, but it felt good blowing free.

Randy turned to face me and reached out to tuck a strand behind my ear. I started to put my hood back on, but he stopped me. "You look great with the ocean behind you and your hair flying," he said.

Our eyes met and held, and then he took my hands in his. Randy's eyes were exactly the color of the ocean. After what seemed like an eternity, he bent over and kissed my lips softly. I held my breath, hardly able to believe this was really happening. Then he pulled me into his arms, oblivious of the surfers below. I could feel my heart pounding against his. As he started to kiss me again, we were interrupted by an announcement over the P.A. system.

"We have the results of heat one . . ." Randy raised his head, listening, ". . . and advancing to the next round . . . third place—Murray, second place—Neuman, and finally . . ." The announcer's voice paused and I shared Randy's tension. "In first place—Randy Harris."

I gave him a hug, burying my face against his soft sweatshirt. "You did it! I *knew* you'd win!"

He laughed. "This is just the beginning. There are two more heats before the finals. It gets a lot harder as you advance." Looking down at me, he said, "You brought me luck, Little One."

"You didn't need luck," I protested. "You were the best!" The expression in his eyes sent warm prickles through me, and I wished this moment could last forever—just the two of us with our arms around each other.

A helicopter flew overhead checking the traffic on Pacific Coast Highway. Above the drone of its motor Randy said, "Kristy, the surfing team is having a party next weekend. Could you . . . would you come—you know, with me?"

I realized he was asking me for a date, a real honest-to-goodness date! "I'd love to," I whispered. I couldn't believe this, either. I had a date with Randy Harris!

A horn sounded and he turned back to watch the next six surfers scramble for the water. His face was rapt with attention on the action below. "You really do love surfing, don't you?"

For a minute he didn't reply. Then he said slowly, "Yes, I really do. It gets to be more than a sport . . . sort of like an addiction. You can't get enough of it." He hesitated, then went on, "When you're out there alone on your board, you can feel the power of the sea. And when you're sitting there waiting to catch a wave, it's a good time to think—to sort through things."

This was a side of Randy I sensed he didn't reveal to most people, and I was happy that he had opened up to me.

Then he shook his head and grinned, blushing a little. "Sorry to ramble on like that. I'd like to teach you to surf someday, Kristy, maybe in the spring."

"I'd like that," I told him, glad that he planned to be around in the spring. "That is, if I have time after gymnastics—"

He put his hand over mine. "We'll find a way to squeeze it in."

"I'm seriously thinking of quitting," I blurted out. Then I caught my breath, realizing that it was the first time I had admitted that to anyone besides myself.

Randy stared at me. "You're kidding! How come?"

I shrugged. "Gymnastics takes up every minute—I don't have time for anything else. You and Michelle got parts in the play, and I couldn't even try out. And I miss all the dances and parties. . . ."

"Whoa!" He put his hands on my shoulders and held me at arm's length. "You've got fantastic talent, Kristy. When you're out there doing your thing, you explode like a sky full of fireworks. I can tell how much you love it. How could you give all of that up?"

"I just feel like I'm missing out on so much."

He thought for a minute. "Sometimes it costs a lot to follow your dream. But it's your decision, Kristy. Just don't settle for less than the best."

His words left me even more confused. Here I was so close to my goal, yet hesitant to claim it. What was wrong with me? It had to be love, I decided. The only thing that mattered right now was being with Randy, but I couldn't tell him that. Then I thought about what he had said about following my dream. Was that one of the reasons he liked me? Would he stop liking me if I gave it up? Why did I feel so good and so rotten at the same time?

*   *   *

That afternoon Michelle came over to my house, and I told her everything that had happened.

"He *kissed* you? Right on the *pier*?" she squealed. "And you're going with him to the surf team party? That's fabulous!"

I grinned. "Yeah, it is, isn't it?"

"How'd Joe do in the meet?"

"He came in third in the first heat, but he got knocked out in the finals." I flopped down next to Michelle on the bed, and when she gave me one of her know-it-all smiles, I was sure she had something she was itching to tell me. "You're holding out on me," I accused. "I told you my big news—now you tell me yours."

"Actually, I've got *two* things," she said.

"Good or bad?"

She rolled over, grabbed a pillow, and started pounding me with it. "*Good*, you idiot!"

"Okay, okay!" I giggled. "Just tell me." Before she could clobber me again, I somer-saulted off the bed. Bubbles, who had been sound asleep on the rug, sprang up and began barking at the commotion.

Michelle threw herself on her stomach and leaned over the edge of the bed, looking at me where I lay on the floor. "Are you ready?"

I nodded. "Go ahead—shoot."

"Joe asked me to the Snowflake Ball last night!"

"The Snowflake Ball!" I jumped to my feet. "Wow! After only one date!" Staggering around the room, I pretended to feel faint.

Michelle sat up, crossing her legs Indian style. "Actually, I gave him a little help," she admitted.

"What'd you do? Tell him you just happened to be available on the seventeenth of January?"

Michelle giggled. "Not exactly. Yesterday afternoon I saw him talking to Alison and some of her dopey friends. Then in French class, Alison hinted to me that Joe might take *her* to the dance. She must have known that I like him. Was I ever green—bright neon-sign green!"

"You know how she is," I said. "Alison wants every boy anyone else wants."

"Anyway," Michelle continued, "when I saw Joe after class, I told him I'd seen him talking to Alison and wondered how the decorations for the ball were coming along. So he kind of stuttered around a little and then he finally asked me!"

"You're so lucky!" I wailed, sitting down on the bed. Michelle would be off dancing with the boy of her dreams and I'd be in L.A., going to bed at nine o'clock because Flip believed his gymnasts should get lots of sleep the night before a meet. Yuck! Gymnastics was definitely ruining my life.

Michelle hugged me. "I wish you could go too," she said.

"So do I," I said sadly. Oh, well—at least I was going to a party with Randy.

"I've got some more news you may like even better," Michelle added. "You know that job you wanted me to help you find?"

"Did you hear about anything?" I asked eagerly.

Michelle grinned. "Did I! I almost had to take it myself. While I was at the beach after school . . ."

"The beach?" I squealed, then lowered my voice to a whisper. "Is there a job at the beach?" Since I wasn't going to tell my family about getting a job, I didn't want to blow it now.

Michelle said, "I went into the pizza place to grab a slice on my way home. It was jammed. So," she continued, looking very satisfied with herself, "I told the lady who owns the shop that it looked like she needed some part-time help. That was when she told me I could start immediately!"

"Did you tell her about me?" I asked eagerly.

Michelle nodded. "I told her you'd be in tomorrow to talk to her."

"Oh, Chelle!" I cried. "Thanks so much! You're the best!"

"What are friends for, anyway?" She rolled off the bed. "But I don't know how you're going to handle it, with school, gymnastics, and everything else."

"I'll work it out somehow. Don't tell anyone about the job, okay? I'm so excited!"

I gave Michelle a hug. Now I could help with my gym fees until I made up my mind whether or not I was going to stick with gymnastics.

Chapter Nine

Sunday afternoon I stopped outside Pizza-by-the-Slice and peered into the window to look it over. I had been in the store many times as a customer, but never with the idea of working. I could see a gray-haired lady wiping off the white counter. Taking a deep breath, I pushed the door open. "Mrs. Locke?" I asked, glancing down at the slip of paper Michelle had given me. "I'm Kristy Warner. I'm here about the job."

The woman smiled at me. "C'mon in. I was hoping you'd show up."

"My friend told me you needed someone," I said.

"Your friend told *me* I needed someone!" She laughed and asked me to sit down at a small table in the corner. She came around the counter to join me, and we began to talk. I explained that I wouldn't be able to work every weekend because of the upcoming gymnastics meets, but that was all right with Mrs. Locke. When I left three hours later, I had the job and had served hundreds of slices to people leaving the beach for the day. I was sure everything would work out great. Now all I had to do was keep all the different parts of my life separate!

Arriving home, I heard the phone ring. Mom picked it up and handed it to me a moment later. "A boy," she whispered, covering the mouthpiece and raising an eyebrow.

My pulse started pounding as I thought, *Please let it be Randy.*

It was. "Hi," he said. "Uh—I—uh—was wondering if you have the homework assignment in algebra."

I couldn't help grinning. He had actually called me, even if it was only for an assignment! I knew Mom was watching from the kitchen door, so I sat down at the table and tried to act casual. "You're in luck. It's a fairly easy one."

"That's good. Uh—did you really enjoy the meet yesterday?"

"I loved it! And your winning the first round made it terrific."

"I had some good waves," he said modestly.

Fifteen minutes later when we hung up, I realized he hadn't mentioned the algebra assignment again. That meant he had just used it as an excuse to call. A smile crept over my face. I wrapped my arms around myself and twirled around in the kitchen, much to Mom's amusement.

All the following week you could feel the tension in the gym. I knew Flip wouldn't let us relax until the first Elite Trial was over. And he would definitely come unglued if he knew that I wasn't all that excited about going. There didn't seem to be any way to explain how I felt, so I kept my feelings locked up inside, going through the workouts without much enthusiasm.

"Kristy!" Flip yelled at me across the room on Thursday evening. "Pick up that run! You look like you're out for a Sunday jog!"

He didn't miss a thing. My concentration had certainly been slipping. All I could think about was Randy and the way he had kissed me on Saturday. I could hardly wait to go to the surf team party with him. It might not be the Snowflake Ball, but it was a start. Michelle and Joe were going too.

Looking at the clock again, I breathed a sigh of relief. Only twenty minutes left. After floor routines I was free, and by then Randy would be here to start vacuuming. I smiled at the thought.

I hadn't noticed that my music had started until Flip came over and scowled at me. I motioned to Angel to start it again but Flip stopped her. "What's with you tonight?" he asked. "And for that matter, all week?"

I shrugged, feeling a little guilty. "I don't know. I just can't seem to concentrate on anything lately."

"Well, you'd better get your act together. This is no time to be slacking off. If I didn't know better I'd swear you were trying out a new clown routine! This is not a circus, Kristy."

"I really don't know what's wrong. Maybe I'm just tired," I said, using the excuse that always worked with my parents.

"Then start going to bed earlier," Flip snapped.

Shifting uncomfortably, I scuffed my foot on the mat. I didn't have anything to say.

Flip sighed. "Kristy, after eight years of working with you, I think I can tell when you're holding out on me. Come back into the real world, the world of hard work. We've got a meet in two weeks."

"I know. I'll try," I murmured.

Flip went to start the music himself. "Let's see that floor routine again—this time with feeling!"

Pushing all my thoughts about Randy away, I went through the routine, ending my last tumbling run with my double full twist. As I held my ending pose I knew it had been good. I glanced over at Flip, waiting for his reaction.

But all he said was, "Practice them all that way. It'll make the difference in Oakland," and he stalked back to the bars.

When workout finally ended, I scooted upstairs to change and collect my books. On my way back down, my heart leapt as I saw Randy come in and start to vacuum. The noise of the heavy-duty motor roared through the gym as I walked over to him. *"Hi!"* I shouted in his ear.

"Hi, Kristy!" he yelled back.

I yelled over the noise of the vacuum, *"As a cleaning lady"*—Randy switched off the motor—*"you look great!"* The last part of my comment echoed in the sudden silence. Flip looked over at me and my team members who were on their way out the door burst into laughter.

From the back of the room, one of the girls called, "He sure *does* look great!"

"I think so too!" another girl said, giggling.

"Oooh, he's gorgeous!"

Angel put her hand over her mouth to keep from laughing and fled from the gym. Flip raised an eyebrow and disappeared into his office.

Face flaming, I ran out the side door.

Randy followed me, calling, "Kristy, wait!"

I ran down the dark driveway and slumped against the low wall in front. Nobody had heard anything but the last of what I'd said. What a dope I had been! I'd probably embarrassed Randy to death.

"Kristy?" Randy spoke softly in the near darkness behind me.

"I'm—I'm sorry," I stammered. "I didn't mean to embarrass you."

He sat down next to me. I stole a quick glance at him and saw that he was smiling. "Before you ran off I was going to ask if you thought I'd look better in an apron," he joked.

My heart lifted. At least *he'd* heard every-thing I had said. "I feel like such a jerk!"

Randy reached out for my chin and raised my face toward his. "I don't think you're a jerk. I think you're fun. And we're both going to have a lot of fun at the party on Saturday." He leaned over and kissed both my cheeks. Then his lips gently brushed mine.

The honk of a horn brought me back to my senses as Dad's car pulled up by the main entrance. Randy whispered, "I'll call you," and I ran to meet my father, the softness of Randy's kiss still warm on my cheeks and lips. My dream of becoming a gymnastic champion seemed less important than ever.

Saturday night I dressed early and waited in the living room for Randy to pick me up for the surf team party. Lori kept peeking out the window while Mom and Dad looked in from the kitchen every five minutes. I don't know who was more excited about my first date, me or my family.

Finally he arrived, right on time. After introducing him to my parents, I went with him to his car. Laughing, Randy opened the passenger door for me and said, "I feel like I've been through an inspection!"

"They all wanted to meet you," I told him. "Lori hasn't been able to hold still all day."

He started the engine and pulled away from the curb. "She's a cutie. Did you look like that when you were her age?"

"All but the freckles." Suddenly tongue-tied, I tried to think of something else to talk about. Maybe I should have made another list.

"Michelle and Joe had to go early," Randy said. "Joe's helping to cook the burgers."

"Yum! I'm starving!"

"Joe said they'd be worth waiting for." Randy pulled into a parking spot between several other cars in front of a big, brightly lit house. "Here we are!"

Inside, we soon found Michelle, and I managed to ward off hunger pains by helping myself to chips and dip while Randy said hello to some of his teammates. I looked around. Everyone there was either a member of the surfing team or one of their dates. I was proud to be there with Randy.

"Joe's cooking." Michelle nodded toward the patio.

Just then the door to the patio slid open and Joe came in with a large tray piled with barbecued hamburgers and toasted buns. "Come on, everybody—chow down!"

We all piled our plates with more chips and pasta salad and heaped the burgers with catsup and relish. Then Randy grabbed two Cokes and led me to a spot in the crowded living room where we sat on the floor and shared a corner of the coffee table.

"This looks delicious," I said, reaching for my giant hamburger.

Randy looked around the room as he munched on a handful of chips. "Looks like the whole team is here." His gaze came back to me and he smiled. "I'm glad you could come. I was afraid you might have to practice or something."

I laughed. "Even Flip isn't so cold-hearted that he'd make us practice on Saturday night."

"I'll remember to keep my Saturday nights free from now on." Randy put an arm around me just as I took a big bite of my burger. Catsup squirted in all directions. "Oh, no!" I cried. "Did I get it all over you?"

Choking back his laughter, Randy shook his head. "No, it looks like you kept it all on your face."

The other kids around us were roaring as I reached for my paper napkin.

"Here, let me." Smiling, Randy took his own napkin and started gently cleaning off my face. "This is a little more makeup than you need. Hey, hold still!" Our very first date, and already I had made a pig of myself! Randy would probably never ask me out again. But he didn't seem to mind. In fact, he acted like he was enjoying himself.

"Hey, that looks like fun," Michelle said, pausing to watch. "I think I'll go spill some catsup on me. Where's my date?" She moved off to find Joe.

Laughing at her comment, we finished our dinner and this time I managed to keep everything inside the hamburger bun.

After we finished eating, some of the guys set up a huge screen and a projector. "We rented a surfing movie," Randy explained. "I hope you like it."

The lights in the living room were turned off and we all settled down to watch the surfers ride giant waves from New Zealand to Hawaii. Randy was particularly interested in the shots of the Bonzai Tube in Hawaii, where the surfers are practically inside the wave. "I'd like to go over there sometime and be good enough to give it a try," he whispered to me.

About halfway through the film, Randy put his arm around me and I rested my head on his shoulder. I hardly remember the rest of the movie—my pulse took off, beating hard the way it did when I had just finished a floor routine. My mind was completely centered on how warm and strong he felt, and how good his after-shave smelled. I couldn't concentrate on anything but Randy and his nearness.

When the movie was over, everyone talked about surfing and how the pros handled those big waves.

"I went to Hawaii one time on a family vacation," I offered. "It was great! We watched some guys really shred the waves . . ."

"You've got to be kidding!" one of the surfers said with a grimace. "You really *enjoyed* a family trip?"

"It wouldn't be a vacation if I had to go with my parents," the only girl on the team added.

Annoyed, I got up and walked away from the group. I had always liked to go places with my family—we had a good time together. But it was obvious that the other kids thought it was dumb.

"It's okay." Randy had followed me and now he grabbed my hand. "Don't let them get to you. They're just mouthing off." He led me over to a small sofa on the other side of the room where we both sat down. "I think it's nice that you and your family take vacations together."

I forced a smile. "My dad had a grocer's convention in Hawaii, so he took us all with him. Mom helped pay for it—that was when her shop was making money."

Randy was silent for a minute. Then he said, "You really are lucky, you know? My dad's always so busy he doesn't have time for vacations. Sometimes my mom used to go with him when he went on a business trip, but my sister and I never got to go."

Just then, Michelle and Joe came over and we talked together until it was time to leave. I felt more comfortable with them than I did with the other kids.

Randy drove me home and parked in front of the house. We talked some more before he walked me to the door. On the porch, he stood looking down at me.

"It was great," he whispered as he bent to kiss me good night. He didn't mention anything about next week, but I hoped I would be part of his Saturday nights from now on.

Chapter Ten

Two weeks later I looked down from the airplane window, following the markings of the San Andreas Fault along the golden, sunburned coastline. I could see the ocean in the distance as we flew toward Oakland for the first Elite meet. I was really excited—in the flurry of getting ready for the trip, I'd almost forgotten how unsure I was about continuing gymnastics.

"Where are we?" Angel leaned across me to peek down.

I shook my head. "Beats me. It all looks the same from up here."

"How come your folks aren't going?" she asked. "They were so excited about the meet."

Sighing, I settled back in my seat. "They wanted to come, but money's a little scarce right now. My mom's shop lost a lot of customers when the new mall opened."

"That's too bad," Angel said sympathetically, then reclined her seat and started leafing through a *Seventeen* magazine.

Reaching in my pocket, I felt the envelope Flip had handed me this morning. Randy had made a special trip to the gym and left it on his desk. I pulled out the folded piece of paper, and read the words for at least the twenty-fifth time:

Kristy,
   Good luck in your meet. I know you can do it! I'll be rooting for you from the beach.

                                    Randy

The note was very special to me. Of course, it would have been nice if he had signed it "Love," but at least he was thinking about me. I put the note back into the envelope and tucked it into my pocket before Angel looked up from her magazine. This was something I wanted to keep to myself. I was sure it would bring me luck.

*   *   *

My teammates and I were waiting for the music to start so we could begin our march into the auditorium. I thought we all looked sharp in our new navy sweats trimmed with red and white.

This was it—the finals, the day I had been working toward for so long. In spite of all my indecision lately, it felt good to be there.

"I can't believe we're here, Kristy!" Angel whispered from behind me. "I can hardly stand it!"

The music began and we were on our way. The minute we walked through the door and onto the auditorium floor, the crowd began to cheer. We lined up in front of the audience as the announcer introduced us.

"Kristy Warner—American Gym Club—Sea-gate, California."

As I stepped forward and raised my hand high, a surge of pride rushed through me. This was almost as good as the Olympics! Here I stood with fifty-eight other hopefuls, all of whom had put in the same number of hours, the same amount of dedication, and made the same sacrifices. We wouldn't all make one of the coveted thirty spots on the national team, but at least we'd gotten this far.

I looked at all the different leotards and

unknown faces. Previously our team had competed against other girls from southern California, but these gymnasts were from all over the country. This competition had given my team a chance to see how good they really were.

The evening sped by. By the time I'd finished vault I'd moved into eighteenth place with the floor exercise coming up next. Beam would be my last event for the night, and hopefully my best.

The first notes of my music for floor exercise came from the loudspeaker and I ran onto the floor. The dance movements had to be sharp, yet graceful. I finished my opening and lined up for my first tumbling run. My first somersault in the air seemed okay but when I hit the mat, slightly back on my heels, I felt an excruciating pain shoot through my left ankle. I fought for control, but as I took the first step into an Arabian cartwheel, I pitched forward onto the mat.

Flip reached me in seconds and began examining my ankle, which had already begun to swell. Leaning back on my elbows, I gulped breaths of air, fighting the tears that filled my eyes. Even Flip's gentle touch felt like knife blades. Far off in the background, I could hear the announcer discussing what I had done wrong.

Helping me to my feet, Flip scooped me up in his arms and carried me off to a chair on the sidelines. Quickly he wrapped my ankle with an elastic bandage.

"That will have to hold it until we get some ice," he said, patting me on the head.

I tried to get to my feet, but Flip gently pushed me back and lifted my leg onto the chair next to me.

"Should I take the back tuck out of the beam routine?" I asked. "It might be safer to do it that way."

"Kristy, you're not going to do any more," Flip said firmly.

Pretending I didn't hear him, I raced on. "I can go right from the walkover into . . ."

"You're not going to compete anymore tonight. I'm scratching you from the meet."

"No!" I cried above the music. "I can't quit now! I've almost qualified!" Eight years of hard work—now this!

Flip shook his head. "We can't take a chance on a permanent injury."

The rest of the meet dragged on. When it finally ended, Angel had made Elite, the first step of her dream of being an Olympic gymnast. For years we had planned that it would be the two of us together. Now, wrapping my arms around myself, I felt an unforgettable stab of envy.

The following day we flew home. After Flip helped me out of the car, all I wanted to do was see my family and go to bed.

The front door burst open and Lori came running toward me. "Kristy's home!" She threw her arms around my waist, almost knocking me off balance. "Are you okay?"

Flip pulled her away. "She'll live. Help me get Kristy inside, Lori. We need to get this foot up."

By then Mom and Dad were at the door and everyone helped settle me on the couch. Dad gave me a hug. "Tough luck, babe."

Mom tucked pillows under my ankle. "How bad is it?" she asked Flip.

"Just a sprain." Flip stood looking down at me. "I think we can have her ready for the next trial."

I squeezed my eyes shut. Just a sprain! Easy to say when you weren't the one in agony. Right now I didn't care if I ever went to another trial. I was sick to death of gymnastics!

After Flip left, Mom sat down at the end of

the couch. For some reason she looked happy. I couldn't quite understand it, the way my meet had gone. Maybe the pain medicine I had taken a while ago was finally taking effect, giving everything a rosy glow.

Smiling, Dad said, "Your mother has some great news, Kristy!"

I tried to think what it might be, but it was the wrong time for guessing games.

Mom smiled too. "I found a space I can afford to rent at the mall—I'm moving the shop."

"That's great, Mom," I mumbled. The mall . . . I tried to concentrate, but tonight I just couldn't focus on the changes the new location would bring. But anything that made Mom happier was fine with me. "That's really good news." I closed my eyes. The medicine was doing its thing and now I just wanted to sleep. . . .

For three days I stayed home with my ankle elevated on a stack of pillows. Flip called several times, but most important, I had heard from Randy on Monday. He was worried about me, and we talked for forty-five minutes. Today he was stopping by to visit me, and I counted the minutes until he came. I was all alone in the house—Mom had been at the shop all day getting ready for her move to the new mall, and a neighbor had dropped Lori at the gym after school. It was so quiet that I could hear the mantel clock tick off the seconds.

"Bubbles!" I called, and was rewarded with a flash of white fur and ten pounds of terrier landing on my stomach as I lay on the couch.

"Oof!" I gasped. "Where have you been?" I nuzzled him against my cheek. "Randy's coming over this afternoon," I told the dog. "He said he'd come straight from drama class. No play practice today."

I looked at the clock again and put Bubbles down on the floor. I was as ready as I would ever be. If I brushed my hair anymore, it would probably fall out. My pink lip gloss had been freshened every ten minutes for the past hour. Tucking my yellow shirt more securely into my pants, I wriggled to a sitting position so I could watch the street from the window.

Finally, fifteen minutes later, I saw Randy. I smoothed my hair again and using the coffee table as a prop, I lurched to my feet and reached for the crutches. It was a pretty awkward passage across the room, but I had just enough time to catch my breath before he rang the bell.

"Hi, Randy," I said as I opened the door. "Come on in."

He looked at me balanced on my crutches, and I saw the concern on his face. For some ridiculous reason, tears welled up in my eyes. I wanted to throw myself into his arms and sob.

Randy saw my tears. Maybe he even read my mind, because he reached out and gently wrapped me in his arms, crutches and all, whispering against my hair, "Kristy, I'm so sorry. I know how much that meet meant to you."

I wanted him to hold me forever. "Thanks, but . . . well, I have another chance—if I want it."

He looked at me in surprise. "Why wouldn't you want it?" Glancing down at my ankle, he released me. "We'd better get you off that foot."

Randy helped me back to the couch and gently placed my ankle on the pillows. I moved over so there would be room for him to sit beside me.

"How's everything at school?" I asked.

"I had a test in chemistry, and algebra's . . . well, it's boring."

"Boring?"

"I miss you, Kristy. Nobody's there to keep

things lively—like rolling Kissing Potion under my seat." He grinned when he saw me blush. "Nothing but plain old equations."

I smiled. "The doctor said I could come back to school tomorrow. Maybe just half a day."

"Would you like me to drive you home?" Randy offered.

"Could you? That would be terrific!" My thoughts raced. I didn't have workout, although Flip wanted me back at the gym for strength and flexibility exercises as soon as possible.

"Stay off that foot in the meantime," he said. "I want you to last at least until noon tomorrow."

"I think I'll be able to make it," I told him. I knew that I would last till noon no matter what.

Leaning back against the sofa pillows, I looked up at Randy. "Mom made lemonade for us. Can you get it?"

"At your service, m'lady."

I pointed to the kitchen door and he went through, returning with a tall glass for each of us. He sat down on the couch next to me.

"How's the play coming?" I asked after we had taken a sip. "Are you enjoying it?"

Randy nodded. "It's going great. It takes a

lot of time, though. But I don't have to tell you about time commitments, do I?"

I laughed and we talked for an hour until he said he had to leave. "You look kind of tired. I'll let myself out. Just take care, okay?" He gave my hand an extra squeeze, then bent down and kissed me lightly on the cheek.

Holding my hand against my cheek, I watched him from the window until he turned the corner. Randy missed me in class. He would be driving me home. My world suddenly looked brighter. Maybe hurting my ankle wasn't the worst thing that could have happened after all!

Chapter Eleven

I had almost forgotten my job, but as the weekend neared I wondered how I could possibly handle it. My ankle felt better. I could stand on it, and even walk around a little without the crutches. My daily trip to the sports doctor to get ultrasound treatments had really paid off, but it was Michelle who came up with the answer as to how I would get to the pizza place.

"What if I pick you up after I'm finished with coaching the Rainbow Team?" she suggested. "We'll tell your mom I'm taking you to the beach, which will be the truth. And I'll pick you up when you're done."

I hesitated. "Do you think she'll let me go?"

"With your trusty friend Michelle? Come on, Kristy! Of course she will."

"You sure you can get the car?" I asked.

She smiled smugly. "I already asked."

On Sunday afternoon three weeks later, I propped my foot on a chair in the pizza shop after work as I waited for Michelle to pick me up. I hoped she wouldn't be late. These Saturday and Sunday afternoon trips to the beach already had Mom suspicious. If she hadn't been so absorbed in setting up her new shop in the mall, she would probably have discovered I was working.

It had been hard at first, but I spent most of my time at the cash register, which meant that I didn't have to hobble around much. At least I had had a week of rest before I was expected to work. The ankle was responding well to the treatments, and I didn't need crutches anymore.

Seeing Michelle pull up to the curb, I walked to the car, limping only a little, and got inside.

"When do you start full-time at the gym?" she asked.

I had been going to the gym for a short

time each day. Flip insisted I keep up with pull-ups and strength exercises so I wouldn't lose muscle tone. "Pretty soon," I replied.

"Excited?"

From her tone of voice, I could tell Michelle sensed my lack of enthusiasm. "Well, I'm not too thrilled about going back," I admitted. "I don't know if I really want to keep up with gymnastics anymore."

"What *do* you want?" She stole a quick glance at me.

I sighed. "I wish I knew! More free time, I guess . . . for activities at school . . . and Randy."

Michelle turned down my street and cautioned, "Don't rush into anything."

"I've really liked this taste of freedom, even if I haven't been able to use it to the fullest." I made a face at the elastic bandage wrapped around my ankle.

"Just think about it awhile, promise?" she said, pulling into my driveway.

I eased myself out of the car. "Thanks for everything, Chelle. I'll think about it."

Michelle didn't realize that I *had* been thinking about it practically every waking hour. And the more I thought about it, the more depressed I became. These last three weeks had been wonderful. I had had plenty of time to spend with Randy, and with Michelle and my other friends as well.

But Monday I was expected back at the gym for half workouts. Flip wanted to find out how much pressure my ankle could take. If I let it, gymnastics would soon eat up every minute of my precious free time. What was I going to do?

I went to workouts all week but I didn't push myself. There were times when I caught Flip watching me quizzically. Did he suspect how close I was to giving up gymnastics? I knew I owed him an explanation, but I wasn't quite ready to say the words that would end the path I had been on for eight years.

But my first day back coaching the Rainbow Team was terrific. Michelle and I started teaching the kids a new routine on the mini-trampoline. While one line of girls bounced on the trampoline and did low dive rolls onto the mat in one direction, girls from the other side did high dive rolls over them. It looked spectacular for such a simple maneuver.

"Kristy, I've got to leave soon," Michelle said after about an hour. "Mom's counting on me to go to that ceramics show with her."

I gave her a playful shove. "Go on. We're almost done."

"Are you sure you can get to work by yourself okay?"

"Of course. I'm taking the bus." I sounded more confident than I felt. This would be my first trip alone since I had hurt my ankle. "I don't have to be there until three—the crowds are thinning out this late in the year."

"Okay. See you."

A few minutes later, Flip poked his head out of the office. "Can you lock up today, Kristy?"

"Sure," I answered. "We're almost through."

"Got a few errands," he said at the door before he left.

When the session was over, I dismissed the girls. While I was saying good-bye to Lori and her friends, I noticed Randy had arrived. He waved as he vacuumed under the beams and bars, and when the last little girl had left, I walked over to him.

"It's good to be working with the Rainbows again," I said.

Above the roar of the vacuum, he just grinned at me.

"Can't you shut that thing off for a minute?" I yelled.

"What?" he shouted back. "And interrupt my career preparation?" He began frantically vacuuming around my feet. "I'm studying to be a cleaning lady!"

"Turn that monster off!"

Randy pretended to be offended. "Monster? This is high-tech equipment! Now you've hurt its feelings." He grinned at me again with a mischievous light in his gray-blue eyes. "And it's coming to get you!"

Randy charged at me with the vacuum and I jumped out of the way, squealing, "Hey! All I wanted to do was talk!"

"It's too late for talking!" He pursued me across the gym. "The man-eating vacuum is out for revenge!"

"Stop it!" I giggled and scampered away. "You just want to sweep me off my feet!"

"And that's exactly what I'm going to do." He hurled himself at me like a rhino on a rampage, running around me in circles, the vacuum wobbling erratically in front of him. I managed to leap out of his way in spite of my ankle. If Flip could see me now, I thought, we would *know* I was procrastinating about coming to full-time workouts.

"Look out!" Randy yelled. "The monster is going to eat up your toes!"

"Oh, yeah? It'll have to catch me first!" I laughed and ran for the bars, flipping up and straddling one of them.

Randy rushed toward me, the vacuum weaving around the equipment. I jumped down and dashed back to the floor-exercise area, laughing hysterically, and Randy continued the chase.

Suddenly he whirled around in one quick motion and wrapped the cord of the vacuum around my feet. I tried to keep my balance, but his surprise attack combined with my weak ankle toppled me over.

The smile immediately left his face and his eyes widened in fear. "Kristy? Are you okay? Did I hurt you?" He switched off the motor and sat down beside me on the mat.

"I'm fine," I said, wiping away tears of laughter. "You're really sneaky, you know? Don't you ever give up?"

Randy shook his head. "Nope. It's tenacity! Don't you think that's a good trait for a cleaning lady?" he said, smiling. Then his expression softened as he added, "And with tiny gymnasts."

He gently pulled me to a sitting position next to him. After the noise of the vacuum, the silence made even our hushed voices seem loud. Randy drew me closer, his eyes never leaving mine. I felt reality slipping away. The gym disappeared and I was suspended somewhere in a floating soap bubble.

"The man-eating vacuum always gets its

prey," he said softly. "Now that I've captured its victim, I can—"

I interrupted him. "Maybe the victim wanted to be captured."

"Then let's call this my prize."

I closed my eyes as he leaned forward to kiss the tip of my nose. Then he kissed my eyelids. I shivered at the sensations those kisses created inside me, and when he finally touched my lips, it was a soft caress, so gentle—almost imagined, almost magical—that it made my heart shudder.

"Kristy," he murmured, holding me in his arms. "This is the grand prize."

I snuggled against the soft flannel of his shirt, my pulse pounding.

Breaking the spell at last, Randy got up and pulled me to my feet. "C'mon, I'll put the monster to bed and we'll go get a soda."

I sighed, reluctant to come back from my dream world. Why did real life have to intrude? But, I realized, as long as Randy was a part of it, real life wasn't so bad after all!

"Kristy? Is that you?" Mom called from the kitchen, when I got home from work that afternoon. "Come in here, please. Your father and I want to talk to you."

"Sit down." My dad pointed to the opposite end of the table where he and Mom were sitting. Dad cleared his throat and came right to the point. "One of the neighbors saw you today working at that pizza joint at the beach—after your mother told you not to get a job."

Feeling guilty, I lowered my eyes. "I—I just wanted to help with the gym bills."

"Kristy, I said we'd manage," Mom interrupted with more sympathy than I expected.

"I know," I said quickly. "But with the shop not doing well, I knew it had to be hard on you both, paying for my lessons and Lori's too."

Mom exchanged a look with Dad.

"We want you to quit the job," Dad said, then waited for my reaction. Actually, I was relieved. It would be one less commitment to worry about, and I'd have more time to be with Randy.

"Okay, I'll quit," I said after a moment. "The busy season is over anyway. I only had a couple of weekends left."

Dad said, "What we're really concerned about is your going right out and doing something you were asked not to do."

"I'm sorry," I mumbled.

Mom leaned across the table. "We know

118

you meant to do a good thing, Kristy. Just try to remember that your parents sometimes know what's right for you."

Dad arched an eyebrow at Mom but he didn't argue, and I was relieved. At least I hadn't been grounded! We talked for a while about Mom's shop, which she expected would start making a profit again after the move, and then I escaped from the kitchen, snatching an orange on the way upstairs. Lori's bedroom door was open and when I stuck my head inside, I saw her sitting on the seat in the large bay window. She looked sad.

"Lori? Are you sick?" I asked.

She sniffled. "No, I'm okay."

I went into the room, moved her feet, and sat down next to her. "Then what's the matter?"

She turned to me. "I want to do something to help with the shop, but everybody leaves me out. Can you think of something I could do?"

I tried to think of something, but my mind was blank.

Lori bit her lip. "Dad said something about balloons when Mom moves to the mall. Maybe I could help blow them up."

Balloons? What did Mom need balloons

119

for? I thought for a minute, then it came to me. "I bet they're going to have a grand opening!"

"Is that a party?" Lori asked, smiling now.

"Yes, that's a party."

"With ice cream?"

I laughed. "I wouldn't be surprised. If only there was something we could do to make it extra special. . . ."

Suddenly I had a great idea. The Rainbow Team! Why couldn't they put on a demonstration to celebrate the opening? I had been looking for some place for them to perform. "Lori, what about the Rainbows doing a show outside Mom's shop?"

She clapped her hands. "Oh, could we, Kristy? That would be great!"

"We'll have to see what Mom thinks, and ask the people at the mall if it's okay."

"Let's go ask Mom now!" She bounded toward the door, full of energy again.

Lori was so excited about the Rainbow Team's demonstration that she hardly stopped talking about it all week. Mom and Dad had agreed it would attract a lot of attention to the new shop, and Michelle had said she would help. I was glad because it would give me more time to spend with her. I hardly saw Michelle these days because she was always at the theater, rehearsing for the play.

The gym was a real grind now that I was back for full workouts. Sometimes I felt I wanted to keep striving for my goal, and other times I just wanted to run out of the gym and never come back.

On Friday I saw Flip glaring at me, so I hurried to the floor-exercise area to work on my tumbling runs with Angel. My ankle no longer twinged each time I landed—the doctor said it was completely healed.

"What's wrong between you and Flip? He's been glowering at you all afternoon," Angel said, wiping her face with a towel.

I sighed. "I think he can tell I haven't been giving one hundred percent. Somehow I don't seem to have the same amount of desire as I did before the accident."

She motioned for me to go next. "It's pretty obvious. We've all been worried about you. You're never going to be ready for the next Elite Trial if you don't get your act together. You've just got to make it, Kristy."

It seemed like everyone was pushing me, trying to substitute their desire for my lack of it. I told myself it was great that the team cared. I couldn't let them down. "I'll try," I mumbled without a lot of enthusiasm.

When I finished beam and all my strength exercises, I was relieved that it was over, at least for today. Without my job, a whole weekend of freedom stretched before me.

"Kristy, may I see you a minute?" Flip called to me as I headed for the locker room.

"Sure." I went into his office and when I saw the look on his face, I knew I was in for it.

"I'd like to know who you're trying to fool out there?" Flip snapped.

"What do you mean?"

"Kristy, I've worked with you for eight years. When I see you making only a token effort, I know it."

"But my ankle . . ." I began.

He cut me off. "Don't give me any garbage about the ankle! You're not working up to potential, and you know it."

I stared down at the floor, unable to deny Flip's accusation.

"This is an all-or-nothing business, Kristy," he went on. "You're going to have to shape up and give it everything you've got or get out."

"I don't know what I want to do," I confessed miserably. "There are just so many things that I don't have time for with gymnastics."

Flip's eyes narrowed and all trace of friendliness vanished. "Either you're a gymnast with the drive it takes to succeed, or you're wasting my time and you should quit."

Tears welled in my eyes. "But I don't . . ."

"Forget the tears! They won't work on me. It's your decision." He walked me to the door. "Go home, and come back when you've made up your mind." He pivoted sharply and stormed back into his office.

"Flip!" I wailed.

He leaned back out. "Michelle can take the Rainbows tomorrow," he said, firmly shutting the door behind him.

I stood staring at the closed door, feeling as if a whole part of my life had been slammed in my face. Running into the locker room, I let the tears pour down my face as I changed into my street clothes. Then I fled out the door toward home, gulping down big sobs.

Chapter Twelve

Saturday morning I didn't even feel like getting up. I wanted to cry but there were no tears left in me—I had soaked my pillow with them the night before.

First, I had been furious at Flip for his lack of support and feeling for me. I was so angry I wanted to throw things, so I picked up one of my fluffy bedroom slippers and threw it at the mirror. It just slid down, knocking over a bottle of nail polish. I couldn't even have a decent temper tantrum.

After a while I felt a little better. Quitting was obviously for the best and I had a brief period of elation. No more workouts—no more pressure—time for school activities and Randy. . . .

But the new feeling didn't last long. I had spent too many years on gymnastics for this to be easy.

I had phoned Michelle Friday night and told her all about it. She'd been sympathetic, but there was really nothing much she could say.

My parents hadn't helped much, either. After I told them, Mom kept heaping sympathy on me. I had thought that was what I wanted, but it only made me feel worse. Dad just looked puzzled and confused, as if he was trying to understand but couldn't.

As for Randy, I couldn't face telling him what had happened yet, so when he called on Saturday I said I was sick. My performance must have been pretty good because he stopped by Sunday afternoon with a rose from his sister's garden. Mom took it and brought it up to my room.

"Kristy," she said, "don't you think you'd better face the world again?"

I shook my head. "I don't want to face anyone . . . or anything."

She sighed. "Life goes on, honey. If you're sure about quitting gymnastics, then start thinking about getting involved in some new activities."

But the problem was that I *wasn't* sure.

Why didn't everyone leave me alone? I just wanted to wallow in my own misery.

Monday morning I gritted my teeth and went to school. Telling Randy that I felt too wobbly to go to the gym, I met four of the girls from my English class at the Taco Bell. The rest of the week I pretended to go to the gym. I hated deceiving Randy, but quitting seemed like letting him down too. I didn't want him to call me a quitter.

By the end of that awful week, I was no closer to making a decision.

On Friday night, the phone jarred my thoughts. It was Michelle. "Kristy? Got time to talk?"

"Yeah, I've got a lot of time these days." I sighed.

"I'm sorry I couldn't do anything with you this afternoon. With *Annie* opening so soon, we're always having extra rehearsals."

I smiled to myself, thinking that she sounded like me not too long ago. "That's okay, Chelle. I'm glad you called."

"What have you been doing with all your spare time?"

"Not much," I answered. "I haven't even seen Randy because he's tied up in rehearsals too."

"Did you go to that meeting of the decorating committee for the Snowflake Ball?" Michelle asked.

"Yeah, but Alison and her dippy friends jumped all over me when I made a suggestion, so I'm not going back."

Michelle was silent on the other end of the line. "Actually," I said, almost to myself, "I have too *much* time now."

"You haven't told Randy yet that you're not going to the gym?"

I let out a long breath. "Nooo . . . I know I've got to tell him soon."

"Why don't you call him now? I almost said something about it at rehearsal."

"Maybe I will. Catch you later."

I hung up and dialed Randy's number, but no one answered and I was relieved. I hated having him think less of me.

At nine o'clock the doorbell rang. A moment later Dad called, "Kristy! Someone to see you."

I peeked down the stairs and saw Randy. Darting back into my room, I gave my hair a quick brush and applied a rosy lip gloss and some blush to cover my paleness. Then I forced a smile and went down to meet him.

But Randy wasn't smiling. He looked over at my dad. "Do you mind if I take Kristy out for a while, Mr. Warner?"

Dad glanced at his watch. "No. But bring her back by ten-thirty, no later."

"You'd better get a sweater," Randy said to me. "It's chilly out." From the equally chilly tone of his voice, I could tell he knew I had left the gym.

In silence we drove to the beach. Randy found a parking spot and stopped the car.

"Come on, let's go for a walk." He grabbed my hand and led me onto the sand. We were the only people there—few were willing to brave the cold for a night walk.

When we reached the water's edge, Randy stopped, watching the black waves rolling in to crash at our feet.

"Why didn't you tell me you'd quit gymnastics?" he asked softly. I could hear the hurt in his voice.

"I didn't want you to know because I wasn't sure I *had* quit," I said. I felt terrible. "Actually, Flip told me to go home and not come back unless I was ready to start working hard again. And I haven't gone back, so I guess I'm not ready."

Randy looked out toward the lights of an oil rig anchored offshore. "You couldn't trust me enough to tell me that?"

My stomach knotted up and suddenly an overwhelming feeling of guilt hit me. "Trust?"

I repeated. "It wasn't anything like that. I just didn't want you to know how weak I'd become. I still can't make up my mind whether I want to stay with the gym program or not."

"Is it because of your injury?" he asked.

"It wasn't just that. I started thinking about quitting gymnastics long ago. Before I got hurt—even before I met you." I smiled a little. "But you helped it along a little. I wanted to have more time to be with you."

Randy stood quietly looking out over the ocean again. Then he turned back to me. "You once told me you had a dream. What happened to it?"

I couldn't answer.

We stood there a long time, his arm wrapped tightly around my shoulders. I rested my head against him, trying to remember when things had started to go wrong. What had happened to my goal? My thoughts drifted back to the time when gymnastics was the most important thing in my life. I recalled the feeling of exhilaration when I made my first full twist, and the sense of pride when I finally mastered my first aerial on the beam.

Randy broke the silence. "Sometimes it takes a lot of work to make a dream come true. Only you can decide if it's worth it."

I thought about his words all the way home. He dropped me off twenty seconds before my curfew, so we said a quick good night. Wanting to be alone, I made a fast escape to my room.

I hardly slept at all that night, thinking about what Randy had said about my dreams and goals, then trying to weigh all the alternatives.

Had I really missed that much? Had I over-rated how much fun everyone else at school was having? The fun times seemed to be only punctuation marks in a kind of long, dull sentence.

Sleep finally came in the early hours of the morning, and I hardly knew where I was when I woke up.

I opened my eyes and blinked. Suddenly I realized that I had made my decision. I was going back to the gym to let Flip know I was ready to make up for lost time—if he would have me, that is.

I bounded out of bed. I really don't know the exact moment I had decided to return to gymnastics, but the important thing was that my decision was made. I was ready to pursue my dream again. But would Flip take me back?

*   *   *

Randy drove me to the gym on Monday after school and wished me luck. "You look a little shaky," he said when I made no attempt to get out of the car.

"I feel like I'm about to battle a dragon," I confessed.

He leaned over and kissed me on the cheek. "Then put on your armor and go get 'em!"

I smiled weakly and slowly got out, watching his car until it was out of sight—anything to postpone facing Flip. But I knew the time to do it was right now, before I chickened out.

When he saw me standing in the door of his office, Flip looked up. Immediately he scowled, his mouth a firm, hard line. He obviously wasn't going to make this easy for me.

I took a deep breath. "I want to come back," I said softly, almost in a whisper.

"You do, eh?" He studied me, and I tried not to squirm under his scrutiny. "How do I know you're back for good? Gymnastics takes dedication. You know that."

I nodded. "I'd still like to be more active at school," I said honestly. "But there'll be a lot of time later for that kind of stuff. Right now, I'm ready and willing to work."

"If you're serious, then welcome back. But

don't think it's going to be easy," Flip warned. "You have a lot of work to make up. Think you can handle it?"

I nodded. His smile relieved the tension inside me, and I threw myself into his arms. "Thanks, Flip! You won't be sorry, I promise!"

He gave me a brief hug and then held me at arm's length, grinning. "I'm glad you came back," he said. "I couldn't believe you were going to throw away all those years."

"I almost did, but someone helped me straighten out my priorities," I said, thinking of Randy.

"Okay!" He gave me a little shove. "Get out there and start making up for lost time!"

I made a fast exit. It felt good knowing Flip was happy to have me back. And I knew Randy would be there to give me a nudge if I ever started having doubts again.

I worked extra hard that night trying to show Flip I meant business. Randy didn't vacuum because he had a late play rehearsal, so I had to wait until the next day before I could tell him the news.

I saw him coming down the hall. He waved and when he reached me, he took my arm and led me toward our algebra class. "He took you back," Randy stated with no question.

I stared at him. "How'd you know?"

He dumped his books on the desk. "I just knew. You're too good not to be given a second chance. Are you glad to be back?"

"It feels great!" I smiled up at him. "Thanks."

"Don't thank me, Kristy," Randy said seriously. "It was your decision, not mine."

I slid into my seat. "It'll mean a lot of work, but I figure it's the same as having a job. If I were working, I'd have to put in a certain number of hours."

"The play is almost like a job . . . only a lot more fun." Randy reached over and took my hand. "And somehow we'll make time for each other, no matter how busy we both are."

"I know. Now that I have my head straightened out, everything's going to be fine."

Mr. Laird came into the room just then and began to call roll. Even algebra didn't seem like such a drag today. After all, it had brought Randy and me together. And it looked like everything was going to work out well.

Time raced by as I devoted myself to preparing for the second Elite Trial—my last chance this year. I stayed late at the gym many nights, practicing long hours under Flip's supervision.

Whenever we could, Michelle and I got together to plan the demonstration for Mom's grand opening. Lori was all excited, and the rest of the Rainbow Team's enthusiasm made Saturday practice sessions a lot of fun.

Randy took me home from the gym on Tuesdays and Thursdays after he vacuumed, and he encouraged me until my confidence soared. It seemed like I had finally balanced both my worlds.

One Thursday night we left the gym a little earlier than usual, so we drove along the beach before going home. It was too cold and windy to walk on the pier so we just sat in the car, watching the waves lit up by the moonlight that filtered through fast-moving clouds.

"Uh . . . Kristy, there's something I've been wanting to ask you," Randy said after we had sat for a while in silence. He put his arm around me and drew me close to his side.

I gazed up at him. "What is it?" I asked. I was sure that whatever it was, my answer would be *yes.*

"Well, you know the Snowflake Ball's coming up on the seventeenth of January," he began, and my heart leapt in my chest. "And

I was wondering—well, I was wondering if you'd like to go with me. If you don't already have a date, that is."

I was so happy I thought I would burst. The boy I loved had actually invited me to the biggest dance of the school year! It was a dream come true! Snuggling closer to him, I whispered, "Oh, Randy, I'd love to go with you. Even if someone else had asked me, I wouldn't have wanted to go with anybody but you!"

He kissed me then, and it wasn't until much later, when I was dreamily getting ready for bed, that I remembered the Elite gymnastics meet in Los Angeles. There was no way I could get out of going. But how could I tell Randy that I had to break our date for the Snowflake Ball?

Chapter Thirteen

A week from Saturday was Mom's grand opening. Randy picked me up in Flip's van that we had loaded with gym equipment on Friday afternoon. His light blue shirt made his eyes seem more blue than gray, and every time I looked at him a warm, happy feeling came over me.

"Hey!" He reached over to open the door. "You look real sharp in those sweats."

I looked down at my navy top and pants trimmed in red and white. "A little advertising for the club."

"Everyone will sign up." He flashed me a smile and started the van.

"Someday I'll get all dressed up and you won't know me," I promised.

Randy laughed as he pulled into traffic. "You'll get your chance at the Snowflake Ball."

The Snowflake Ball! A feeling of dismay swept over me. I still hadn't been able to face telling him that I wouldn't be able to go. I would have to tell him today, right after the demonstration was over.

When we got to Mom's shop, Michelle was already there with the team. Each girl wore a red or blue leotard with long silver fringe sewn into the seams down the sleeves. Fascinated with the way the fringe moved when they waved their arms, the girls twirled and spun. They all looked adorable, but I thought Lori looked cutest of all.

With Dad's help, it didn't take Michelle and me long to arrange our equipment. Randy hooked up the record player and microphone to an amplifier Dad had rented.

The girls and their costumes had already attracted a lot of curious passersby, and many found their way into Mom's shop. When I caught Mom's attention, I waved and pointed at the door, calling, "We're about ready to start."

I returned to the roped-off area and stepped up to the microphone. "I'd like to welcome all of you to a gymnastics demonstration," I began. "It's sponsored by Coffee Delight, the new shop right behind me, where you can find super gifts or just relax with a cup of coffee and homemade pastry."

People began to gather around, and I was thrilled. If they all went into the shop after the demonstration, Mom's grand opening would be a huge success.

At my signal, the girls ran out, their silver fringe sparkling under the lights. Their somersaults and flips were greeted by bursts of applause. After a dive-roll contest over the large padded block, the girls lined up for their routine with the mini-trampoline. As they went through their paces, the long fringe fluttered from their outstretched arms.

When the last three girls finished with aerial somersaults, the applause thundered. The girls' flushed, happy faces and the delighted smiles of the audience gave me goose bumps. It had been worth all the effort!

"Wow!" Randy turned to me in amazement. "Those kids were fantastic!"

I beamed with pride. "They sure were."

"You have an hour before the next show."

Randy grabbed my hand. "Let's go walk around. Michelle went Christmas shopping."

I looked at all the little gymnasts standing around us, hanging on every word. "We can't just leave them."

"You're right," he answered. "We'll take them with us."

"You're crazy!" I laughed.

"You may be right." He motioned for the team to follow us. "Come on, gang! We're going for a walk. Stay together now."

My idea of a nice walk with my boyfriend didn't include sixteen little girls trailing after us, but Randy started off, pulling me along.

At least with the girls along, he wouldn't be bringing up the Snowflake Ball—I hoped. The show had taken my mind off the dance for a while, but now I had to think of a way to tell him I couldn't go because I would be at the Elite meet.

At one point we encouraged the team to play around the large sculptures placed in the center of the mall for children to climb on. We sat down on a bench nearby and I decided I had to tell him about the ball right now before I got cold feet.

"Randy . . ." I began.

"Don't say anything," he interrupted, and

reached into his pocket, pulling out a small box wrapped in red paper. "I was going to save this for a special moment, but I can't wait any longer."

He handed me the package and I swallowed hard. No boy had ever bought me a present before! Unwrapping it carefully, I tucked the paper and ribbon into my sweats pocket. I wanted to save every part of his gift. Then I lifted the lid, and saw a small gold locket on satin lining. "Oh, Randy!" I whispered. "I love it!" I knew I would wear it forever. I threw my arms around him, forgetting about the shoppers, the bright lights, and the little girls. "Thank you!"

He kissed me, then took both my hands. "I wanted to give you something as special as you are," he said.

"What are you guys doing?" Lori asked.

Another girl chimed in, "Is it time to go back?"

I looked up to find the team surrounding us. This may have been a special present, and a special time for Randy and me, but it certainly wasn't very private!

We did two more shows, each one drawing a bigger crowd, and most of the spectators went right into Mom's shop. She was so busy that Dad and Michelle pitched in to help her wait on all the customers.

After we had everything secured in the van, Randy and I took cups of Mom's orange cinnamon tea and found ourselves a bench in the mall.

"You and Michelle did a great job with those kids, Kristy," he said.

"Thanks." I sighed, happy that the demo had been so successful, but also glad that it was over.

Randy put his arm around me and pulled me close. Just being with him made me feel relaxed and happy. I would have to tell him about the dance soon, but not right now. Maybe tomorrow. . . .

As we sipped our tea, Randy said, "Hey, Kristy, I forgot to tell you—some of the guys on the surfing team have been asked to form a kind of honor guard for the queen of the Snowflake Ball and . . . well, I'm one of them. That means I'll have to leave you alone for a while. Is that okay?"

My stomach knotted up and my mouth felt dry. Why hadn't I told him before?

Randy grinned. "You should see the look on your face! It won't take more than about fifteen minutes. I'm not going to run off with the queen or anything."

I turned away and looked at the floor.

"Kristy? What's wrong?"

I blinked away the tears that filled my eyes. "Randy, that's the night before the Elite meet."

"No problem. We won't stay late at the dance."

I shook my head. "You don't understand. Flip never lets us go out the night before a meet, and besides . . ."

I couldn't go on. My throat choked up and tears began to trickle down my cheeks.

"If you tell him how much it means . . ."

"Randy," I said around the lump in my throat, "I won't even be here. The meet is in Los Angeles. We leave Friday afternoon."

He stared at me. "Oh, great! I can't believe it. The biggest event at school and my girlfriend can't go. Why didn't you tell me before? I thought you'd stopped keeping secrets from me!"

"I meant to tell you, honestly I did. But I was so thrilled when you asked me to go that I just couldn't say no. Oh, Randy, you knew I'd have to give up some things when I went back to gymnastics."

"But the Snowflake Ball isn't just *anything*."

"Neither is the Elite meet," I choked out.

"It's what I've been working toward my whole life."

"I know that," Randy said. "I just don't see why you can't leave the next morning. And I don't understand why you said you'd go when you knew you couldn't." He looked away. "Maybe I should take someone else."

"Well, maybe you should!" I was getting angry now, probably because I felt so guilty. The minute the words were out of my mouth, I wished I could take them back. But it was too late.

Randy stood up and glared at me. "If that's how you feel, maybe I will!" He turned and stalked away. I watched him until he was swallowed up in the crowd. He didn't look back, not even once.

Chapter Fourteen

The following days, my life seemed empty. I missed Randy so much, and the thought of his taking another girl to the dance made me feel awful. I had come to think of him as mine. How wrong I had been!

Hard work was my only relief. The long hours I spent on my training impressed Flip, and I knew I had more than made up for lost time. My determination to place in this meet kept me going—except at school.

The last two weeks before winter vacation, Randy and I went through the halls pretending not to see each other. He even ignored me when we sat next to each other in algebra. If only he could understand why I had to go to this meet! I wanted to try to explain, but my pride wouldn't let me. Once I caught him giving me a hopeful look when our eyes met, but I turned away quickly. I couldn't let him see how crushed I felt.

Usually after algebra I would gather my books and bolt out the door, but one morning I held back, letting Randy leave first. I watched him from behind, thinking how appealing the back of his head with the familiar dark hair curling at the nape of his neck looked. I knew how soft and silky it felt. . . . But that was over. All I had left was the memory.

When I reached the door, I saw him standing in the hall with Alison, who smiled sweetly up at him. Obviously, she had been hanging around, waiting for our class to end.

Seeing me, she sent a scorching look my way before turning to Randy again, her sweet expression dropping quickly back into place.

Randy saw her glance at me and turned. "Kristy," he started. "I . . . ."

I didn't wait to hear what he was about to say. Abruptly brushing past them, I raced down the hall. I couldn't stand to see them together. If only these last few days of school would end! Vacation couldn't get here fast enough.

One day during lunch hour Randy cornered me at my locker. Trying to steady my uneven breathing, I snapped my lock shut and turned to face him.

"Can't we even talk?" He reached out and touched the chain that must have been peeking out from my collar. I wore his locket every day, hidden under either my sweater or blouse. Even in my misery I couldn't leave it in my jewelry box.

"What's this?" he asked, pulling the locket out.

I pushed his hand away. "What's to talk about? Nothing's changed." I choked on the words. "I still can't go to the Snowflake Ball."

He reached out to touch the locket again. "I know, but . . ."

"Randy!" a sugary voice called.

We looked up and saw Alison coming down the hall. When Randy turned toward her, I raced off toward chemistry class. All I seemed to be doing lately was running away. I didn't want to, but I couldn't seem to help myself. I just couldn't stand to see the two of them together. It hurt too much. Couldn't he see my heart was breaking?

When vacation finally arrived, I divided my time between long workouts at the gym and helping at Mom's shop with the large Christmas crowds. I tried not to ruin the holidays for my family, gritting my teeth and forcing myself to smile, but in spite of my pretense, everyone knew that Randy and I had broken up, and I could feel their sympathy.

By the time Christmas vacation ended, I was so sick of pretending to enjoy myself that even school sounded good. But the prospect of seeing Randy again made me want to stay home. By the time I got to school, I was a nervous wreck. In algebra class, Mr. Laird gave us a review sheet that took the whole hour. There was no opportunity to talk with Randy even if I had been able to think of anything to say.

The next day Michelle and I found a sunny corner in the quad to eat lunch. Michelle leaned back against the building fidgeting with her lunch bag, obviously ill at ease.

Finally I said, "Out with it, Chelle. What's wrong?"

She looked over at me and sighed. "I hate to be the one to tell you, but I don't want you to get it from the school gossips. . . ."

A warning bell went off inside me. "Randy?"

"He asked Alison to the Snowflake Ball. I'm sorry, Kristy."

I felt like I had been run over by a train. How could he do this to me? I didn't really expect him to stay home, but of all the girls he could have invited, Alison was the worst.

Michelle looked as sad as I felt. "Don't worry, Kristy," she said. "Randy's too nice a guy to put up with her for long."

I choked down the rest of my lunch and spent the last of the hour in the library, trying hard not to cry.

On January sixteenth, my heart as heavy as lead, I went with Flip and the other members of the gymnastics team to Los Angeles. But I wasn't going to let thoughts of Randy ruin my chance to make the Elite gymnastics team. While I did my warm-ups the next day, I forced myself to concentrate on the little things that would put the extra touches on my routines. Even if I was a loser in love, maybe I could be a winner in gymnastics.

As I finished up on the balance beam, a flash of color caught my eye and I whirled around. Somebody was standing in the doorway of the huge gym, trying to untangle an enormous bouquet of red, white, and blue balloons. I caught my breath. It looked like— but it couldn't be! What would Randy be doing here? I must be seeing things!

Then the guy started coming toward me and I realized that it *was* Randy. Our eyes met and I forgot all the hurt. I just wanted to see him, talk to him, and touch him.

When he reached me, he didn't say a word. He just slipped the plastic bracelet that held the balloons onto my wrist. We looked at each other in silence for what seemed like ages. Finally Randy spoke. "Kristy, I acted like a real jerk. I'm so sorry," he whispered.

"How could you take Alison to the Snowflake Ball?" I burst out, resisting the temptation to throw myself into his arms.

Randy reached out and took my hands. "After you told me you couldn't go, I wanted to talk to you, but every time I tried, you ran away. I thought it meant you didn't care about me anymore. Then I saw you wearing my locket, so I figured maybe you did. But you still shut me out."

"But Alison . . . of all the girls to ask! Why her?"

He shook his head. "*She* practically asked *me*. I didn't realize . . ."

"How I might feel?" Now that I had started, I knew I couldn't stop. "First you encourage me to go back to the gym, and then when it interferes with a school activity, you drop me for that—that *airhead*!"

Randy looked sheepish. "I—I guess I wasn't prepared for your gymnastics to interfere with the biggest dance of the year." Then he smiled a little. "You're right about Alison.

She doesn't have much in the brains department. The dance was miserable. Alison was so boring that I even considered going home and leaving her there. She was so busy flirting with all the other guys, she probably wouldn't have noticed."

The idea of Alison finding her date gone brought a tiny smile to my lips.

"Of course, I didn't. I couldn't do that to anyone," he went on. "But I wanted to. And I missed you every minute. That's why I got up at dawn and drove here—to tell you."

If my heart had been heavy before, now it was soaring like the balloons attached to my wrist. He cared! He really did!

"Please say we can forget these past few weeks and start over—together," Randy said softly.

I felt my eyes fill with tears, but these were tears of joy.

"Kristy, what's wrong?" Randy asked.

"I'm just so happy you're here!" I cried.

Randy put his arms around me. "So am I. I love you, Kristy," he said right before he kissed me.

Suddenly aware of the giggles of the other gymnasts, I pulled away. "The balloons are terrific," I told him. "But I'm going to have trouble doing my routines with them."

"I'll hold them for you," Randy offered.

I shook my head. "No way! I'll tie them to my gym bag. I want to keep them with me for luck."

"Good luck, Kristy." He planted a kiss on my nose, then hurried to take a seat. I had a tough job ahead of me, but now that Randy would be waiting, I felt I could conquer anything!

By the time I had finished my floor routine and marched to the balance beam, I knew that I was doing better than I ever had before. But would it be good enough to make the team? Each girl in this meet was competing for the same few spots and they were *all* good.

I awaited my turn anxiously. My new double-back combination had to be perfect and I could feel the tension mounting. Maybe I should have kept the old routine and not given myself more difficulty.

I shook my head to clear my doubts, and stepped forward to salute the judges, knowing that every bit of my concentration must be focused on my performance.

My feet floated above the beam and my heart was thrilled at the extra height I reached with my split leap. Then the moment arrived for the move that would either help me score high enough to qualify or send me back for another year of training.

I threw myself into the air, my eyes trained on the center of the narrow strip of wood. When I landed solidly I could hardly contain my joy. I went into my dismount, and the crowd cheered and applauded. Flip sent me back out to wave at the audience, and I immediately looked for Randy. As our eyes met, the rest of the crowd faded away. His smiling face and thumbs-up sign were all I saw.

When the announcer's voice finally came over the loudspeaker, the auditorium became still. Each gymnast held her breath, hoping she would be chosen.

"Ladies and gentlemen, I now give you the National Elite Gymnastics Team. . . ."

When they called my name, I closed my eyes for a minute, hardly able to believe my ears. Then I bounded out to the center of the floor, shivering with excitement. My dream had come true! I was now a member of the small select group of Elite gymnasts! And Randy's presence made it *absolutely* perfect. Though I knew things wouldn't be easy for us, we would work them out somehow. Lots of school activities would still be out for me, and Randy would be awfully busy too. But as long as we cared for each other, we would always manage to take time out for love.